DATE DUE   MAR 0 5

10/27/05			
GAYLORD			PRINTED IN U.S.A.

SIREN'S SONG

*Also by Cathy Forsythe
in Large Print:*

Love Between the Lines

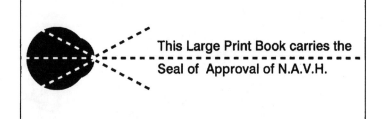

This Large Print Book carries the
Seal of Approval of N.A.V.H.

SIREN'S SONG

Cathy Forsythe

Thorndike Press • Waterville, Maine

Published in 2004 by arrangement with Cathy A. Forsythe.

Thorndike Press® Large Print Candlelight.

The tree indicium is a trademark of Thorndike Press.

The text of this Large Print edition is unabridged.
Other aspects of the book may vary from the original edition.

Set in 16 pt. Plantin by Ramona Watson.

Printed in the United States on permanent paper.

Library of Congress Cataloging-in-Publication Data

Forsythe, Cathy.
    Siren's song / Cathy Forsythe.
      p. cm.
    ISBN 0-7862-7041-1 (lg. print : hc : alk. paper)
    1. Policewomen — Fiction. 2. Police corruption —
Fiction. 3. Brothers and sisters — Fiction. 4. Large type
books. I. Title.
PS3556.O7446S57 2004
813'.6—dc22   2004056740

To Bob,
my very own hero

As the Founder/CEO of NAVH, the only national health agency solely devoted to those who, although not totally blind, have an eye disease which could lead to serious visual impairment, I am pleased to recognize Thorndike Press* as one of the leading publishers in the large print field.

Founded in 1954 in San Francisco to prepare large print textbooks for partially seeing children, NAVH became the pioneer and standard setting agency in the preparation of large type.

Today, those publishers who meet our standards carry the prestigious "Seal of Approval" indicating high quality large print. We are delighted that Thorndike Press is one of the publishers whose titles meet these standards. We are also pleased to recognize the significant contribution Thorndike Press is making in this important and growing field.

Lorraine H. Marchi, L.H.D.
Founder/CEO
NAVH

* Thorndike Press encompasses the following imprints: Thorndike, Wheeler, Walker and Large Print Press.

Chapter One

Kelly was bone weary. With a ragged sigh, she glanced at the battered wall clock. One more hour. Surely she could make it just one more hour. Giving her hand a quick shake to work out the writer's cramp, she bent her head back to the seemingly endless paperwork.

Glancing over her shoulder to check on her prisoner, Kelly found he was fast asleep. Great. He was a good-size man, and it wouldn't be easy to wake him from his drunken stupor long enough to walk him into the jail and turn him over to a booking officer. Sorting through the last of the paperwork, she tucked the bundle of papers under her arm and turned to tackle the last unpleasant job of her shift.

Standing behind the man in case he woke up violently, Kelly bent and began to empty out his pockets. She slipped everything she found into a plastic bag and sealed it.

"Mr. Massey," she called loudly, nudging

his leg with her foot. *Please wake up,* she wished silently.

The man didn't even stir. After trying once more, Kelly put down her papers. She tried to work her shoulder under his arm to gain some leverage. Almost gagging when his sour breath hit her, she backed off to study the situation. She had no choice but to hold her breath. She couldn't stay here until the guy woke up; it could be hours.

After an awkward slip, Kelly pulled him to his feet. Trying to prop him against the wall with one hand, she grabbed her paperwork and his property bag with the other. As she stretched for the door, she spotted a piece of paper sticking out of his pocket.

"Just my luck," she muttered. Now she'd have to reopen the bag and write a report on why she'd missed the paper. She just wanted to go home and get some sleep, not push her aching hand to print another form. Grabbing the paper, she quickly stuffed it in her pocket so it wouldn't be forgotten. This guy was feeling heavier by the minute.

Propping his sagging body against the wall, Kelly began to slide him toward the door. A juggling act was accomplished while she opened the door and eased around it with her burden. She was almost there. Kelly cheered herself on, breathing heavily from the exertion. The paperwork began to fall and she instinctively grabbed for it. As soon as she took one hand away from the man, his body twisted and began to slide. Struggling to regain her balance, she tripped over his foot and ended up in an undignified heap on top of him.

Kelly ground her teeth together to keep from screaming in frustration. The entire shift had been one calamity after another. The scream almost sneaked out again when a pair of polished cowboy boots moved into her view.

"Having troubles, ma'am?"

That was the understatement of the year. Kelly took a moment to glare at the boots. The newcomer bent down to offer her a hand, and she stood slowly. Keeping her head averted to hide the very unprofessional blush on her cheeks, Kelly leaned over once again to drag her prisoner off the floor. Capable hands brushed her aside, and in one smooth motion, her rescuer hauled up her prisoner.

"Better get your papers," the officer reminded her before turning to the booking room and bellowing for them to open up and get a cell ready.

Kelly found herself scampering behind him like an errant child. Quickly turning in her paperwork, she called a thank you to the plainclothes officer and escaped without ever looking at his face.

In the peace of her patrol car, Kelly took deep breaths to calm herself. That had not been conduct becoming an officer of her experience. She'd been with the Jackson Police Department in northern Colorado for five years and she'd never had trouble like that.

Slowly pulling her car out of the jail's garage, she gave a sigh of relief. She had survived her last night shift as a uniformed officer. There were a few times when she'd had her doubts. This last hour had been one of them.

Kelly examined her image in the mirror with a critical eye. A cool, calm, and collected visage stared back. But her insides were in turmoil. She grabbed her makeup and quickly dabbed at the dark circles under her eyes. The change from night shift to day shift had left her a few hours short on sleep, and she needed to look her best this morning. Today, her long-awaited dream of working in the detective division was coming true.

Giving the lacy ruffle at her throat a last twitch of adjustment, she worried again over her choice of clothing. The suit she'd selected was very businesslike and tailored. Years of wearing a masculine uniform made her long for feminine touches in her clothing. In defiance of the image she needed to project, she had chosen a blouse that was all softness and lace to go underneath the suit jacket. Under the blouse she wore her frilly teddy, which made her feel very delicate and ladylike. But all that was well hidden, leaving only a professional shell for the world to see.

Calling for her brother to finish dressing, Kelly hurried to get breakfast ready. A still sleepy-eyed Jimmy followed her at a slower pace.

"Morning, pumpkin," Kelly called as she turned away from the refrigerator, balancing milk and juice.

Jimmy mumbled a response and sat down at the table with a big yawn. "Do I have to go to school today, Kel?" he grumbled, his face twisted into a parody of pain.

Kelly forced away a sigh. This was becoming a daily routine. "Yes, you do."

"I'm really sick today," he wailed, slumping farther down in his chair.

She reached over and felt his forehead. It

was cool, as usual. Frowning, she studied his face. The poor little guy did look tired, but certainly not sick. Deep down she was afraid he still hadn't adjusted to the sudden loss of their parents a year ago. It had been a hard blow to her at the age of twenty-seven. The seven-year-old had a much tougher time.

Straightening, she finally replied, "You've missed too much school already, Jimmy. I'm afraid you'll have to tough it out today. You don't have a fever, and we agreed you'd only stay home when you had a temperature." For once, Jimmy gave in without the usual battle, but he pouted throughout their quick breakfast.

Kelly watched her little brother walk into school with his feet dragging, and she felt a tug at her heart. Suspecting he was trying to make her feel guilty, she turned away and slid into her battered old car. Being at the bottom of the totem pole in the detective division earned her the right to drive the oldest, ugliest car available. She just hoped it wouldn't collapse in the middle of the street without warning.

Staring up at the jagged mountains in front of her, Kelly tried to draw strength from the beauty of the scene. This sight was one of the things that had first attracted her parents to Colorado. She had grown up looking at this majestic splendor and had found many hours of peace tramping through the hidden paths the mountains guarded.

Pulling into the parking lot, Kelly stopped in the only available space. She cast a longing glance at the shiny white Camaro in the next slot as she hurried by. Someday she was going to have a racy sports car like that. Maybe after Jimmy graduated from college, she promised herself. She had too many other responsibilities now.

Thank goodness she was early. The butterflies in her stomach had rested while she concentrated on getting the little boy off to school. Now those butterflies launched into full flight. Kelly took a few deep breaths and stepped into the room, grateful a dozen pairs of eyes weren't turning to study her.

A cup of strong, black coffee was the first order of the day. Kelly headed for the coffee machine, which was placed in a strategic location right next to the lieutenant's office. She silently blessed the kind soul who had come in early and made coffee. The aroma of the fresh brew teased her nose as she crossed the room. She was so

13

absorbed in calming herself with the ritual of getting a cup ready, for a moment she didn't notice the loud voices coming from the office beside her.

"I refuse to work with some undergrown sprout for a partner," a man practically shouted.

"She's not all that little," another male voice responded calmly. "Probably about five-and-a-half feet tall."

Kelly had a sinking feeling this conversation was about her, and she started to move away from the door. She didn't want to be caught eavesdropping.

The first male voice answered, a little louder. "My new partner" — the word fairly dripped with sarcasm — "is a woman, and unless you assigned me an Amazon, she's little. Women generally are. They're also incompetent cops and nothing but trouble."

The other man's reply was muffled as Kelly threaded her way through the desks. She'd almost made it across the room to stand by the windows when the lieutenant's office door was snatched open.

"Like you say, I may have to live with it, but I don't have to like it. That little lady had better have her act together or she won't make it here. I'll see to that." The

14

speaker slammed the door behind him.

Kelly kept her back to the room, staring out the window as she tried to fight her growing panic. She'd fought and won against the stigma of being a woman in the patrol division. After proving herself and being accepted as one of the guys, she hadn't expected to have to prove her abilities again. With a sigh of resignation, she pasted a brilliant smile on her face and turned to greet the man she'd be working closely with. One more battle wouldn't kill her.

Kelly's smile slipped when she saw him standing in front of the lieutenant's office. Being confronted with her new partner almost broke her determination to succeed at this promotion. The man stood with his feet planted firmly apart, thumbs hooked in his belt, while he arrogantly returned her study. His blond hair was every-hair-in-place perfect, and deep blue eyes topped a neatly trimmed mustache. A well-used sheepskin coat was slung carelessly over one arm. Broad shoulders easily filled out a red-and-blue plaid shirt, and a slightly disreputable-looking pair of jeans covered long, lean legs all the way down to a pair of highly polished cowboy boots. He might be considered handsome, but the cynical twist of his features spoiled the effect.

"So, you're the little sprout those idiots upstairs chose for my new partner," the man drawled, crossing the room.

Kelly's temper flared at being called a sprout. Not quite trusting herself to be civil to her new partner, she settled for glaring at him with an intensity designed to melt the wall behind him.

Unperturbed, the man stepped in front of her. "You any good?"

Kelly had been a cop too long to let her emotions show. She wasn't about to let this . . . this *man* get the better of her. With more confidence than she felt, she challenged, "I'm the best. You any good?"

Surprise flickered in his eyes for a moment, soon replaced by a twinkle of amusement. Ignoring her question, he chose instead to study her once more. Taking in the simple black pumps on her feet, Jayk let his gaze slide up a shapely pair of legs to her very proper blue skirt with a very proper matching jacket. The way the jacket hugged her body, he doubted she was wearing her duty gun. Jayk looked again into those beautiful green eyes, which were calmly studying him back. They were surrounded by a soft,

16

creamy complexion and a riot of dark brown curls that he suspected couldn't be tamed.

"Well, sprout, let's get to work," he announced suddenly, spinning away on his heel, ignoring the twinge of masculine interest he felt.

"Excuse me," Kelly called after him. Waiting until he had stopped and turned to look at her, she said, "It would be helpful if I at least knew your name."

"Sergeant Taggert." He dropped into an old chair behind a battered, cluttered desk.

Kelly slowly followed him across the room. No first name. Okay, two could play this game. She'd be darned if she'd call him sergeant or sir. Studying the boots he had propped on the desk, Kelly thought "cowboy" might be suitable. A picture of him riding a galloping horse down a busy city street almost made her laugh out loud.

Not five minutes later, Fillmore came strolling up to the desk with the excuse of looking for a lost report. Jayk suppressed a grin at the other officer's freshly combed hair. Jayk had seen the man use breath spray just before coming over. Fillmore was convinced that all women found him irresistible.

"Your new partner show up yet?" Fillmore asked innocently, studying Kelly out of the corner of his eye.

"Here she is," Jayk replied, waving a hand in Kelly's direction. "Meet Kelly Young, our latest addition."

The other detective immediately came over to shake hands and introduce himself, letting Kelly know very early in their short conversation that he was willing and available. Fillmore was too slick for her taste and she gently put him off, turning her attention back to her new job.

Kelly had her total concentration focused on Jayk's words when someone blocked the sunlight streaming in from the window. Glancing up, she was surprised to see Captain Dunham smiling at her.

"Congratulations on your promotion, Kelly." With a pleased smile, the captain shook her hand. "You deserve it after all those years of hard work." Giving a brief nod to Jayk, the man strode off before Kelly could answer.

After the third interruption, Jayk bounced out of his chair. "Come on, let's get out of here."

Grabbing his coat, he left without checking to see if Kelly was with him. He was already out front, pacing the sidewalk, before she caught up. Without a word, Jayk turned and opened the driver's door of the Camaro Kelly had admired. As she reached for the passenger door, he glared at her over the roof.

"Don't hit the door on anything and make sure your feet are clean."

Kelly fought the urge to slam the car door to release a bit of frustration. She settled for sliding smoothly into the car, closing the door with excessive care, and turning to stare at her new partner.

"How do you rate such a nice car?" she asked.

"I own it." Jayk pulled the powerful car out of its parking place, blending into the busy traffic.

Stopping at a red light, he cleared his throat. "We're going to kind of a rough neighborhood. You do have a gun with you, don't you?"

Kelly's mouth almost dropped open in surprise. What kind of bubbleheaded idiot did he think she was, anyway? Police officers always carried a gun, on duty or off. "Of course I do. I even brought along real bullets, but they're in my pocket so I don't have an accident."

Jayk grunted in acknowledgement as he concentrated on his driving. At least she had spunk. But he'd never feel comfortable with a female partner. Women were too emotional, too unpredictable. Never knowing what she was going to do or how she'd react made his job doubly difficult. A cop needed to know his partner as well as he knew himself. Jayk hadn't met a woman he could get that comfortable with.

Kelly noticed the neighborhood was rapidly deteriorating around her, and she wondered what her new partner was up to. She suspected he'd test her before accepting her.

Parking the car in front of a particularly sleazy-looking bar, Jayk stepped out without a word and disappeared inside. Determined to be included in his work, Kelly started to follow him. Before she got to the doorway, a group of rough-looking boys appeared out of nowhere and surrounded her. With a quickening pulse, she looked at the youthful faces, wondering what they were up to.

"Hey, baby." The apparent leader of the group leered at her. "Whatcha doin' in these parts all by yourself?"

Feeling the veiled threat in the boy's words, Kelly almost forced her way through the group. Stopping herself, she realized a show of confidence was the only way to deal with them. Kelly looked the kid straight in the eye, gave him her brightest smile, and announced in a no-nonsense tone, "Back off, friend, before I have to do something we'll both regret."

The boy blinked, then his face broke into a wide smile. "All right," he said, stepping back with an awkward sweep of his arm, indicating a clear path for Kelly. Clutching her purse a little closer, she hurried past.

Kelly entered the bar and stopped, blinking owlishly while her eyes adjusted to the dark interior. Spotting Jayk through a curtained doorway across the room, she followed, weaving between empty tables. *It just isn't that easy to get rid of Kelly Young*, she thought, almost grinding her teeth in frustration.

As she pushed her way into the next room, Kelly saw Jayk talking with someone in a dark corner. Moving forward cautiously, she was only able to catch disjointed pieces of the conversation.

". . . June fifth then, for sure," Jayk was saying to a man still hidden in the shadows. Jayk glanced around and caught sight of Kelly. "What the —" The other man melted out of sight.

"You're supposed to be waiting in the car," Jayk growled as he took her arm and steered her outside.

"Like a good little girl?" Kelly snapped, shaking herself free from his grip.

"Get going, or you'll ruin everything, you idiot."

Pressing her lips together, Kelly slipped through the curtained doorway. Partners, she kept repeating to herself. They were partners. They had to learn to get along, to trust each other, to depend on each other. Getting into the car, Kelly allowed herself the pleasure of giving the car door a satisfying slam.

Jayk climbed into the car, seething. First, this woman had scared off his informant. Then she had the audacity to abuse his car. Turning to read her the riot act, he noticed her satisfied expression. His temper flaring, he reached out to grab her arm. "What kind of foolish stunt was that?"

Kelly turned and looked pointedly at his hand on her arm. When he finally got the message and released her, she glared at him.

"I thought I was your partner, not your trained dog. Either way, you forgot to command, 'sit, stay' before you left. Last I checked, partners work together, communicate with each other, and back each other up." She emphasized the last few words.

"I don't want or need a partner, especially not a woman," Jayk growled as he put the car in gear.

Biting back the angry words bubbling inside her, she forced herself to lean back in the seat. She needed all the patience and expertise she possessed to get through this. Having fought these prejudices before, Kelly thought she knew what to expect. A sudden wave of discouragement surprised her. In the past, proving herself had been an exciting challenge. Now it made her feel tired. *I must be getting old,* she thought wryly.

As they pulled away from the curb, she saw the gang of boys who had confronted her earlier. They returned her smile and waved, calling after her to hurry back and see them.

Sighing, Kelly waited to see what would happen next. She was a good officer; she was confident she'd be a good detective. Why couldn't these macho male types accept the fact that a woman could do this job? Maybe not with brute strength, but with tact, finesse, and a clever mind.

She looked through the windshield to the mountains displayed against the afternoon sky. Thunderclouds rolled over the tops of the dark peaks, preparing for a typical late-afternoon rain. The familiar view calmed her nerves somewhat, and she slowly drew strength from the soul-stirring sight. She would find a way to get through this. She would make it. She had to.

"Where do you keep your gun?" Jayk eyed her as if she might suddenly grow a set of horns.

"In my purse, for now."

"What if you lose the purse?" He steered around a turning car. "The gun is better in a holster on your body, so it's always available."

Good heavens! The man was actually giving her some advice, even if he was talking to her like an inexperienced rookie.

"In case you hadn't noticed, women's clothes aren't exactly made to conceal a gun. Those delicate little belts they put on slacks won't hold the weight of a gun and these nice tailored jackets don't give enough to go over the top of a shoulder holster. I ran out of ideas after that." Kelly snapped her mouth closed before any more of her irritation could tumble out. She'd wrestled for several days on where to hide her gun. Her purse was the only solution.

Regretting her outburst, she vowed to try to tolerate the cowboy. She'd worked with other men sporting impossible attitudes, and through hard work and dedication she had won them all over eventually. Somehow, Kelly doubted she'd ever gain Jayk's confidence. But she couldn't ask for a new partner already, and she wasn't about to give up the promotion and ask for a transfer. That left few choices.

As Jayk skillfully maneuvered the Camaro through the heavy traffic, he wrestled with his feelings. He didn't trust women in general and specifically not as a partner. Surprisingly, he was almost impressed with the sprout — so far. She was tough, and she gave as good as she got. She acted as if she might even know her job. But she was a woman. Women couldn't be effective police officers. They simply didn't have the right stuff.

Later that night, as the two new partners prepared to leave the station for the evening, someone called Kelly's name.

"Kelly, wait up a minute," a husky uniformed man called.

Her eyes sparkled as she moved down the hall to meet him. "Hi, Russ." As the two met, Russ Burton put an arm across Kelly's shoulders and gave her a little hug. Kelly returned the greeting with enthusiasm.

25

"How's the new detective doing? Showing all those old fogies how the job's done?"

Kelly laughed with delight at his kidding. It had been a rough day, and she needed this from her old friend. Glancing over her shoulder, she saw Jayk stop and raise an eyebrow in her direction. She could just imagine what he was thinking.

When Jayk heard Kelly's name, he paused to watch. Everything he learned about this woman would help him decide how to cope with her. Seeing what he expected, Jayk gleefully latched on to the little scene as further proof that she was just like all the rest. No morals, no scruples, and serious trouble for any male officer within range. Spinning on his heel and heading out the door, he wondered at the vague disappointment he felt at this discovery.

Chapter Two

Kelly sat in front of a manual typewriter, struggling to punch out a report on the prehistoric monster. It was an irritating change from the sleek computer keyboard she was used to. With her tongue clamped firmly between her teeth and her curls falling into her eyes, she hardly resembled a hard-bitten police detective.

The phone rang beside her, breaking her concentration and causing her to hit two keys, jamming them together. With a muttered curse, she reached for the phone with one hand while trying to pry the keys apart with the other.

"I want it back," a gravelly male voice demanded.

Instantly, Kelly tensed, every instinct coming alive. Was this for real or just one of the crank phone calls cops attracted constantly?

"What are you talking about?" she demanded.

"You know what I want. If I don't get it

soon, real soon, someone is going to get hurt."

Before she could ask questions, the caller rudely hung up. She was staring at the phone in confusion when Jayk walked up to the desk.

"Your turn," he said, jerking his thumb toward the lieutenant's office.

"Huh?" Kelly jumped a little, snapping out of her perplexed study of the telephone.

"Lieutenant wants to see you," Jayk explained with a bit of impatience. "He wants to give you a pep talk."

Kelly got up without replying, forgetting all about the odd phone call. Feeling as if she were walking into the lion's den, she kept reassuring herself that she had done nothing wrong.

Straightening the bow on her new pink blouse, Kelly took a deep breath and stepped into the lieutenant's office. "You wanted to see me, sir?" She tried to still the tremble that passed through her. Second day on the job and she was already in his office. Not an auspicious start, to say the least.

Lieutenant Goodman looked up from the papers scattered across his desk and gave Kelly a quick smile. "So you're the one causing such an uproar in my division." He stood to shake her hand. "Jayk whisked you off so fast yesterday I didn't even get a chance to give you my welcome speech. Now I have to put that aside for more important things. Too bad," he added with a sigh. "It's a great little speech."

Suddenly looking more stern and very lieutenantlike, the man leaned forward in his chair. "You're not going to have an easy time working with Sergeant Taggert." The lieutenant pursed his lips as if trying to decide what to reveal next. "He had the misfortune of being involved in a bad situation with a female officer awhile back. As you know, most male officers are pretty distrustful of a new female officer until she's proven herself. I'm not sure that you'll ever be able to win Jayk's confidence."

Pausing again, the lieutenant bounced his pencil on the desk. "I just want you to know that I understand the problem and I'm on your side. But, for reasons of my own, I won't assign you a different partner. Good luck to you, Kelly." The man rose from his chair, ending the meeting.

"By the way," he called as Kelly opened the door. "Captain Dunham tells me you're pretty sharp with computers. Maybe you can give these clowns some training one day. They need all the help they can get."

Kelly smiled in agreement and managed to mutter a quick thank you — although she couldn't think of one thing to actually thank him for — before scooting out the door.

Just wonderful! Her partner, the man she had to trust with her life, hated women cops. He had a problem with them. All because of a "bad situation." That left Kelly with a lot of questions and absolutely no answers. By the time she got back to her scarred wooden desk, she was muttering under her breath about men and their fragile egos.

Jayk looked up from his reading and studied her with one eyebrow cocked. "How'd the pep talk go?" Before Kelly could answer, he continued. "Now you know that I'm a horrible, rotten excuse for a human being, but we're stuck with each other." With a knowing wink, he added, "I tried to wiggle out of the partnership too."

Kelly watched him look away as she sat down at her desk. A friendly word. He had actually completed one normal, civil sentence. Resisting the urge to comment on this turn of events, she swiveled around to finish her report, only to find it gone.

Instead, an odd-looking excuse for a holster sat in the middle of her desk. Picking it up, Kelly realized it was designed to be worn on the ankle. Glancing up, she saw Jayk suddenly become very interested in his middle desk drawer. He kept pawing through it as if he'd lost something.

"Do you know anything about this?" she finally asked, holding up the holster.

"It's for you," he mumbled.

"Is it yours?" Kelly couldn't resist pushing the issue a bit. The cowboy was practically squirming in his chair.

"Yeah" was the only answer she got.

"And it's for me to use?"

Jayk finally turned to face Kelly. "If you could bring yourself to wear slacks to work, you could conceal your gun very comfortably. I think you'd be safer with the gun on your person instead of in your purse. We'll be going into some pretty rough areas, and pants would be more practical anyway. Skirts like the one you wore yesterday are only going to cause trouble." Jayk turned away to continue studying her report. He'd never admit her skirt had caused trouble with his own concentration.

Kelly blinked at him in surprise. That

31

was almost a speech. A nice, caring, concerned speech. Would wonders never cease? There might be hope for them yet. A very slim hope, but certainly more than there was yesterday.

She overcame her shock enough to thank Jayk and ask for her report back so she could finish it. He came over to her desk and proceeded to dissect her report into little pieces. Nothing she'd written seemed to satisfy him, not even the page numbers. *So much for hope*, Kelly thought.

Leaning back in his chair, Jayk watched Kelly through half closed eyelids as she worked on her report. He was deeply entrenched in one of the most complicated cases of his career. More than six months of work were already behind him. He was getting close — he could feel it.

Someone very clever had been rerouting truckloads of merchandise to a bogus warehouse and then disappearing with the goods. Stereos, computers, furniture, even grocery items had been quietly spirited away. All the tidbits he'd picked up through a well-tended string of informants were starting to fit together. But there were still several pieces missing from the puzzle. The biggest questions he'd yet to answer were how and who.

A twisting in his gut reminded Jayk of one path he had yet to pursue. Someone within the department might be involved. There had been indications, but so far he had ignored this possibility. Dirty cops made him physically ill.

How in the devil was he going to tie all this up in a neat little bundle with Kelly tagging on his heels all day? No amount of yelling and threatening had changed the lieutenant's mind about suddenly saddling him with a partner. Having always worked best alone, Jayk wasn't even sure how to work with another person.

He'd just have to find a way to keep Kelly occupied with unimportant details during the day. When she went home at night, he'd get on with the real work. It would make for some long days, but he was getting bored with just his television for company, anyway. The extra work just might be the cure for the odd restlessness he'd experienced lately.

With a start, Jayk realized he'd been daydreaming. Kelly stood in front of him, waiting patiently for him to check her report once more. As he dropped his booted feet from the top of the desk, he let his eyes slide down her trim figure. Jayk shook himself mentally. He didn't have time for this.

Picking up the report, he forced his mind away from the woman at his side and studied the words for a second time. Grudgingly, he admitted the sprout knew her stuff. This was a very well-written document. But he'd never tell her that.

"It'll do," he grumbled, quickly signing his name in approval before shoving it back across the desk.

Kelly hesitated, feeling a trace of awkwardness at the question she wanted to ask. Reaching for the report to stall for time, she fingered it.

"Will you be needing me for about an hour?"

Jayk glanced at her in irritation. Her second day on the job and she already wanted time off. "Why?"

"I am allowed a lunch break if we're not busy." Her words were cool. "Right?"

Surprise crossed Jayk's features. His lunch was usually a hamburger on the run. It had been years since he'd taken his allotted lunch hour, and he'd almost forgotten about it.

"Right," he replied. "Do you want to go now?" He glanced at his watch, surprised at how fast the morning had gone by.

"In a few minutes." Kelly returned to her desk, humming a little under her breath. Glancing at the clock, she saw she had just enough time to freshen up, and she grabbed her purse.

This was probably not the best time to take off for a long lunch, but she badly needed some information. Russ always seemed to know the other officers' deep, dark secrets. She needed some ideas on how to deal with her partner. And Russ was just the person to give her the necessary ammunition.

Jayk watched her exit with interest. She certainly seemed happy all of a sudden. The sprout must be meeting someone special. Turning back to his desk, he forced his wandering attention to the job at hand. It was time to map out what he needed to accomplish this evening. He also needed to think of some busywork for his partner, something to keep her out of his hair for the rest of the afternoon.

Kelly strolled back into the room looking fresh and neat, glancing at the clock once more. Just as she settled at her desk, Russ called out from the doorway.

"I haven't got all day, detective, ma'am." He started laughing at Kelly's indignant look. "Let's go."

Jayk saw her face light up at the sight of the big man. He felt a stab of irritation as she hurried off to meet him. The knife twisted a bit when the two locked arms and headed out the door, laughing together. Why on earth should he care? Now he had time to get some real work done for a change, instead of baby-sitting a rookie.

"Tell me what you know about Jayk Taggert," Kelly asked, carefully stirring sugar into her iced tea. "Why is he so dead set against women?" She looked up to see Russ lean back in his chair and study the ceiling, as if trying to read the answer to her question in the faded tiles.

Kelly smiled fondly while she waited. They had joined the police force around the same time and had struggled through the embarrassment of being greenhorn rookies together. Very early in their relationship, they discovered they'd never be more than very good friends. They got along well and enjoyed each other's company, but the essential spark for a romantic involvement was missing.

Russ was Kelly's private cheering section when she became discouraged about being a woman in a man's world. They had spent many pleasant hours together, honing their shooting and self-defense skills. Russ had taken the time to teach her the small things needed to be a good cop. Things that little boys grew up with and little girls rarely even saw.

"Now don't get your dander up about this," Russ finally said. "I know how you feel about women in police work. All I ask is that you hear me out before throwing a fit."

Kelly gave him a puzzled grin. "Okay, out with it."

Taking a sip of his own iced tea, Russ looked thoughtful for a moment. "Most of this is bits and pieces I've heard over the years." He paused.

Kelly sighed. It could take Russ forever to tell a good story. And she had learned a long time ago it was useless to hurry him.

"Some years ago," he said, "a new female detective came into the division. She was assigned to one of Jayk's good friends, Jim Barry, as a partner. The woman knew her job and had a lot of confidence. Everyone seemed to think she showed some promise and would prove that women could do the job as well as any man."

The waiter came with their lunch and Russ paused in his story. He took several hungry bites before continuing. Kelly picked at her food with a feeling of dread.

His initial hunger satisfied, Russ went

on. "The two worked well together for about a month. Then a drug deal went down unexpectedly, and Jim and his new partner were the only ones available to handle it. Things went bad. The woman panicked and froze up. Jim took a bullet while trying to get his partner out, and he's been paralyzed from the waist down ever since. She never even drew her gun. Jim managed to take the guy out after he'd been shot, or they both would have been killed." Russ watched Kelly for a second, then returned to his meal.

She gave up all pretense of eating. How was she ever going to compete with that? How would she ever be able to do enough to prove herself? She had heard similar stories about male officers, but the tales never caused the same prejudice and distrust as the stories about female officers.

Russ finished his meal and pointed to Kelly's hamburger. "You going to eat that?"

Giving him a slight smile, she shook her head. Her friend grabbed it and wolfed it down as if he hadn't eaten for days. With that finished, he ordered pie and ice cream.

Leaning back while he waited, Russ finally spoke. "Kelly, you're a good officer.

We've been in some tough spots together and you've never once let me down. You've got what it takes, and not all of our male officers can say that. I'd rather have you at my back than anyone else in this department." He leaned forward. "Is Taggert giving you trouble already?"

"He just doesn't trust me," Kelly replied. "Now I wonder if he ever will."

"You want me to have a talk with him?"

Biting back a loud and horrified no, Kelly smiled politely and told him no thanks. Russ, at times, had all the finesse of a raging bull. She'd never stand a chance of winning Jayk over after Russ got finished with him.

Kelly tried to keep up a stream of nonsensical chatter while Russ finished his dessert. She needed to distract him from the idea of helping her out. In the past, even after she'd asked him not to, Russ had insisted on taking care of her in odd little ways. If she had a flat tire on her patrol car, he'd change it for her. One time, when they had to stand out in the pouring rain, he had all but forced his raincoat on her when he found out she'd forgotten hers. These actions frustrated Kelly. But she'd finally learned to accept them gracefully. In the ways that really counted, he treated her as an equal. He was her best friend.

The pair strolled back to the police station in companionable silence, enjoying the warm summer day. Russ walked Kelly to her division and then wished her good luck before departing. She glanced around for Jayk. When she didn't see him, she checked her desk for a note.

A white-hot rage blurred her vision for a moment after she read the terse note on her desk. It told her to file the stack of pawnshop records he'd left for her. This job was normally done by the high school–age cadets when they came in after school. What made that pigheaded cowboy think it was *her* job?

Glancing at the lieutenant's office, Kelly considered stomping over and raising the roof, but she'd always been one to deal with her own problems. Crying to a supervisor every time something went wrong never helped anyone.

Kelly forced herself to calmly pull out her desk chair and sit down. Deliberately picking up a slip, she put it in its proper slot. Soon her nimble fingers were flying through the work, while her mind plotted several horrible fates for one Jayk Taggert.

Looking up from her work several hours later, Kelly realized it was almost time to go home. The expectant hush that came with the end of the day was settling over the room. She slipped the last few papers in place and leaned back to stretch. Blinking a few times to clear the tired burning from her eyes, she grabbed her purse and the holster Jayk had given her. Tomorrow would be soon enough to try to wrestle the unfamiliar thing onto her ankle. It would certainly be a welcome relief to get the extra weight out of her purse.

By the time Kelly pulled into her driveway, she was relaxed enough to be humming a song along with the radio. Strolling over to the neighbors' house to pick up Jimmy, she leaned over and snitched a rosebud from Milly's pampered bushes. How the woman found time to cultivate these beautiful things was beyond her. Raising four kids was enough, but Milly called her gardening recreation.

Kelly twirled the red flower under her nose as she walked up to the spotless house. She loved roses. Someday she'd find the right man and he'd send her baskets full of them. White roses. Laughing at her ridiculous thought, Kelly opened the door and stepped inside.

"Anyone home?" The house was silent, so Kelly went to the back door. As she stepped outside, she caught a flash of yellow out of the corner of her eye. She managed to duck as a water balloon sailed by and splashed against the house.

"All right, give yourselves up," Kelly called. "Come out with your hands in the air."

A moment later, a chorus of giggles led her to their hiding place. She grabbed a smiling Jimmy by the elbow and dragged him out. It was good to see him laughing again. That carefree feeling had been slow in coming back after the shock of losing his parents. In a flash, Kelly wondered if Jayk liked children. Where on earth had that thought come from?

"Well, at least now I don't have to worry about what to make for supper," she teased the squirming boy. "It's bread and water for you, youngster."

Jimmy giggled all the harder as Kelly hugged him.

"I thought I heard a commotion out here." Milly stepped out the back door. "How's the new job going?"

"Fine, I guess," Kelly answered, her smile dimming.

Milly cocked her head. "Now there's an enthusiastic answer if I've ever heard one. Troubles already?"

"Just a chauvinist for a partner."

"Is he young and good-looking or fat and balding?" her friend asked innocently.

Kelly paused to consider. "I guess good-looking, if you like the cowboy type." After a pause, she added a "Whoops!" and glanced at Milly's grinning face. Her husband was one of those "cowboy types."

Jimmy squirmed out of her arms, bellowing that he was starved to death. Walking home hand in hand, they discussed his day. It certainly sounded a lot better than hers.

Kelly slipped two potatoes into the microwave while she put hamburger patties on the grill. She hated to cook that way, but a demanding job left her little choice. Luckily, Jimmy ate just about anything.

After the quick meal, she allowed her mind to slip over her day while she did the dishes. Jimmy was outside taking advantage of the last rays of sunlight. Thinking about the tragic story Russ had related, she felt she almost understood Jayk's feelings toward her. She quickly quelled the rush of sympathy building within her. The very same thing had been known to happen to male officers; panic and fear weren't just female traits.

The slam of a car door brought Kelly's

attention back to the job at hand. The man wasn't worth the time and effort of worrying. Peering through the window, she spotted a white Camaro sitting in her driveway. Her heartbeat accelerating, she moved to the front door.

Just as she opened it, Kelly saw a red balloon sail through the air — straight toward Jayk. A wet splat hit him square in the middle of his chest. Caught unawares, he tucked his head and rolled on his shoulder away from any possible threat. He stood warily, his hand resting on his gun, looking around for a culprit. A sheepish grin crossed his face when he saw the tattered remains of the balloon.

"At least he has a sense of humor," Kelly muttered as she raced out the front door. Zeroing in on the giggling coming from behind a big evergreen, she latched on to Jimmy and pulled him out into the open.

Jayk watched in surprise as Kelly, her hair wilder than ever, came flying out the door and pulled a laughing young boy from the bushes. He felt a sense of disappointment to find that she had a home and family. Her hubby was probably inside reading the evening paper, and a dark-haired little girl was playing with her dolls somewhere.

After a quick word with Jimmy, Kelly turned to Jayk to apologize. Jimmy took his chance to escape.

Jayk held up a hand to stop her words. "I wasn't sure if you'd like it if I came over, but I never expected an all-out war." He laughed and looked down at the damage. "I don't suppose you have a towel, do you?"

Without a word, Kelly spun around and headed into the house, wondering all the while why Jayk was visiting. She was fairly certain this wasn't a social call. And he had been very persistent in not allowing her to participate in any of his work. Grabbing a fresh towel, she hurried out of the kitchen to find him standing uncertainly in the open doorway.

Kelly silently handed him the towel and watched with interest as he sopped up the damp shirt. The drenched material clung tightly to Jayk's muscled chest. A touch of interest ran through her, she noted with surprise. He was a bullheaded cowboy, she reminded herself. There was so much more to any man than just good looks. This particular one also had a bad temper and ill-mannered ways.

Jayk watched Kelly study him with a mixture of amusement and irritation. She was probably sizing him up. He knew her type well enough: all sweetness and nice as long as everything was going her way. But at the first sign of trouble or opportunity, suddenly it was "anything goes."

Clearing his throat, he tried to bring his attention back to the purpose of his visit. After the way he'd treated her for the last two days, he wouldn't blame her if she told him to go jump in a lake. It really rubbed him wrong to even ask for her help at all. Now he'd be forced to disclose a few details of the case.

When Kelly raised questioning eyes to meet his, he dropped his own gaze and shuffled his feet. "I need your help," he finally said. He hated the idea of involving this woman. But, he reminded himself, she would just be a prop. For appearances' sake only.

Kelly felt a ripple of surprise, which was quickly replaced by suspicion. "Need more filing done?" she asked sweetly, barely keeping the sarcasm out of her voice.

Jayk looked a little uncomfortable. "Sorry about that. I had to leave on short notice, and I figured that would give you something to do."

Sure, and pigs fly, Kelly told herself. Hiding her irritation, she motioned him into the living room. "We can at least sit down while we talk. Can I get you something to drink?"

Stepping out of the shower, Kelly let the breeze from the open bathroom window cool her wet skin. The spring days had been unseasonably hot, and everyone was beginning to feel the heat. As she dried off and finished her nightly routine, she mulled over Jayk's unexpected visit.

She had barely held on to her temper while he briefly outlined his plans. Without really telling her anything about the case he was working on, Jayk had asked her to help him with some undercover work. He needed to stay at an exclusive hotel on the outskirts of town for the next two days. In order to give himself a reason to be there, he wanted Kelly to pose as his new bride. This would give them numerous opportunities to sit in dark, quiet corners for hours without raising any suspicions.

Kelly had agreed to the plan, only because it was her job and Jayk was her superior. Maybe it would give her a chance to prove her abilities to the arrogant cowboy. But it would take all her limited acting abilities to be a starry-eyed lover. The cowboy irritated her beyond reason, and she could have trouble playing the part. Of course, it might be fun to smile lovingly at him while she told him what she thought of him through clenched teeth.

Stepping over to her closet, Kelly quickly leafed through her clothing, trying to decide if she had anything suitable. As she looked, her mind played over the rest of Jayk's visit.

When she had stepped into the kitchen to refresh their iced teas, Kelly caught Jimmy trying to sneak in the back door. She'd ordered him to go into the living room and apologize for his actions. Too bad she had to play the heavy. The whole incident had appealed to her sense of revenge — it couldn't have happened to a more deserving victim.

As Kelly returned to the living room, she was surprised to see Jayk and Jimmy sitting on the couch with their heads together. Kelly felt a twinge of jealousy as the two burst into laughter over a shared joke.

When she set down the glasses, she looked at them. "Is this a private joke, or can you share the fun?"

"I was just telling Jimmy about some of my childhood escapades," Jayk answered.

Kelly experienced an unwelcome tug of emotion at the twinkle in Jayk's eyes. The man really should laugh more often. It changed his entire face and made him look downright handsome. Well, almost handsome, Kelly quickly corrected. She didn't want to be attracted to him in any way, shape, or form.

Jayk picked up his glass and took a sip of the fragrant tea, looking around the room. The place had a pleasant, homey feeling to it that was missing in his own house. Eyeing Kelly over the rim of his glass, he asked a little too innocently, "Where's the rest of your family tonight?"

"This is it," Kelly answered with a wave of her hand. "Just Jimmy and me."

At the speculative gleam in Jayk's eye, she couldn't keep the sarcasm from her voice. "He's my brother. What time do I need to be ready in the morning? And what about clothes? Do you have anything special in mind?"

"Be ready by nine. I want to get an early start," Jayk ordered. "We'll need to present an image of being fairly well-to-do. Are you set for daytime fun in the sun and elegant evenings at the hotel?"

Kelly resisted the urge to stuff a pillow in his face, answering sweetly, "I'll try not to embarrass you."

Getting up to leave, he tossed one last

comment over his shoulder. "Don't forget your gun." Kelly gave into the urge and threw a pillow, striking him squarely in the middle of his back.

"Hey, what was that for?" he cried, spinning around.

Kelly was all but sputtering with indignation. "Oh, never mind." She resisted the urge to slam the door behind him.

Double-checking to make sure everything she'd need for the next two days was clean, Kelly gave a tired sigh and crawled into bed. First thing in the morning, she'd pack and be ready to go. Thank heavens for the arrangement she had with Milly. The other woman had wanted a way to make a little money while she stayed home with her children, and Kelly had needed someone who would be available anytime to watch Jimmy. She wouldn't have to scramble to find a baby-sitter on such short notice. Determinedly shutting her mind to any further thoughts or plans, she punched her pillow once and settled down to sleep.

The loud ring of the telephone on her nightstand scared Kelly half to death. Once before, she'd been roused out of a deep sleep only to hear the news of her parents' accident. She reached for the phone and gave a hesitant hello. After a short silence, she heard the same gravelly voice she'd listened to earlier at work.

"Leave it in the bus depot's ladies' rest room tomorrow at ten o'clock. Someone will pick it up. Do it or there'll be trouble."

The phone clicked in Kelly's ear and the caller was gone. Frowning, she slowly replaced the receiver. This guy obviously knew quite a bit about her if he knew her home phone number. It had been unlisted for several years, after she got tired of the occasional weird phone call that seemed to be part of her job. Getting this second call at home was definitely not reassuring. Kelly turned over and punched her pillow. So much for her good night's sleep.

Chapter Three

The shrill buzz of the alarm forced Kelly to bury her head deeper in the pillow. Hadn't she fallen asleep just a few minutes ago? Prying one eye open, she saw the brilliant morning sun creeping around the edges of her window shade. She groaned as she tried to disengage herself from the tangled covers. A night of worrying really messed up a bed. Kelly surveyed the damage but decided she couldn't face anything before her morning coffee.

She'd made no progress in trying to figure out what the late-night caller wanted. Finally, she'd decided to mention the calls to Jayk. Even if he couldn't come up with a reason for them, it wouldn't hurt for someone else to know.

Lying in the dark quiet of her bedroom, Kelly had let her mind drift to her new partner. Worrying about their professional relationship soon turned to wondering about Jayk as a person. When Kelly realized the direction her mind was taking, she scolded herself. Using all the relaxation techniques she'd ever learned, she tried to rest. Finally, she counted sheep, only to see a cowboy on horseback chasing each woolly image.

Squinting against the morning brightness, Kelly padded into the kitchen, thoroughly disgusted with her wayward thoughts. She sat down at the kitchen table and unthinkingly took a gulp of hot coffee. While nursing her burned mouth, she tried to talk herself out of even the slightest interest in Jayk as a man. He was her partner. Nothing more.

She'd seen enough police officers in action to know that a lot of them were party animals. When she fell in love and got married, she wanted a nice, quiet, safe man. Maybe an accountant or an electrician. Someone who loved and respected her. Someone to help raise their children and help care for their home.

A glance at the clock told Kelly she needed to hurry. She still had to pack and then make herself look rich and in love. Makeup might not be enough for the "in love" part, but she had a few pieces of clothing to help her look wealthy.

Quickly going through her closet, she chose a loose sequined blouse and a pair of black silk slacks. Next she pulled out several sundresses. Kelly frowned before throwing them into the suitcase. She'd be forced to carry her gun in her purse. With a devilish gleam in her eye, she threw in her new white swimsuit. She had just enough of a tan to really show it off. Knowing she was out of time, she closed the suitcase and went to wake Jimmy.

His jubilant cry when he heard he could spend the weekend at Milly's house reassured Kelly he wouldn't miss her. She packed a few clothes for him while he collected some favorite toys. After a hurried breakfast, Kelly walked him over to Milly's house, still in her bathrobe.

Hurrying back across the damp lawn, Kelly saw Jayk's car turning the corner. She almost ran into the house, but as he pulled into the driveway, she stood and glowered at him from the front step.

Jayk stepped out of the car, trying to suppress a flash of irritation. She wasn't even dressed yet. If he had to wait an hour or two for her to get ready, it would throw his whole day off. As he let his eyes drift over her sleepy, tousled appearance, his anger faded into a strange warmth. The stirrings were what any normal man felt toward an attractive woman, he assured himself quickly. Trying to call his anger back, Jayk strode toward the house. "Aren't you ready yet?"

Any embarrassment Kelly felt quickly turned to the slow, burning anger she usually experienced around Jayk. "I believe you're a little early," she answered with all the dignity she could muster. That was difficult while standing in wet grass, her feet bare, wearing her washed-out bathrobe. She resisted the urge to run a hand through her hair.

Jayk reached for the screen door and with a sweep of his arm, indicated Kelly should proceed him. "If I could trouble you for a cup of coffee, I'll be as quiet as a mouse while you slip some clothes on."

Kelly stepped inside and led the way to the kitchen, wondering if she had any arsenic. Without a word, she poured his coffee and swept out of the room, determined to get dressed in record time.

Exactly twenty-two minutes later, she entered the kitchen feeling she fit the part she needed to play. Her curly hair was swept back into a long barrette, emphasizing her high cheekbones and sparkling green eyes. She wore a fashionable white suit that highlighted her slim figure and gave her just the proper touch of elegance.

"Ready when you are," she announced. "Not all women need two hours to make themselves presentable."

"Suitcase all packed?"

"Sitting by the front door." Kelly went to lock the back door, then she turned to glare at him. "Are you coming?"

Jayk jumped up with a vague sensation he was losing control of the situation. He grabbed the suitcase and went outside.

Letting a small smile sneak through, Kelly leisurely locked the front door and joined him in the car. She was barely settled in her seat before they roared away from the house.

On the ride to the hotel, she let the scenery wash over her in soothing waves. This was one of her favorite drives. Pine trees contrasted with scattered aspens, while craggy rocks complemented smooth-faced canyons. The tangy freshness of the air was unspoiled by the noise and smell of the city. And to be staying at the Cragmont Hotel was an added treat. The elegant old building was an historic landmark, well-known for its service and ambience. Situated several miles outside of Jackson, the hotel was nestled in a quiet corner of the Rocky Mountains — an added plus for people wanting peace and quiet but convenience too.

As they pulled up under the covered entryway, Kelly pasted what she hoped was a loving smile on her face and waited for Jayk to walk around to open her door. She almost groaned aloud as she watched him settle a gray cowboy hat on his head. His grin indicated he was ready to play his part with enough reality to prick her irritation. Again.

"Come on, honey," Jayk drawled, holding his hand out to her. "Let's check into our room and get comfortable."

Gritting her teeth at the endearment, Kelly slipped gracefully out of the car and reached out to take Jayk's arm. As she touched him, she felt a shiver of sensation begin at her fingertips. The racing current that shot through her arm almost caused her to jerk away. Instead, she smiled a little brighter and tried to ignore her instinctive reaction to the man beside her. This was work, not fun.

Kelly almost lost her cool again when she heard Jayk had reserved the honeymoon suite. It had never occurred to her they'd sleep in the same room.

As they mounted the long, curving stairway, she felt her heartbeat accelerate. It suddenly seemed like the beginning of something. Not willing to acknowledge that her personal life might change, Kelly forced her thoughts to what little she knew about Jayk's case. He'd only told her he needed to watch someone for a few days. It was obvious he only wanted her along as a prop. Maybe, if she kept her eyes and ears open, she'd be able to find out something in spite of him.

Kelly's thoughts were interrupted by the bellboy, who threw open the double doors to their suite. She barely registered the elegant interior before she noticed Jayk watching her with a speculative gleam.

He tipped the bellboy and muttered just loud enough for Kelly to hear, "Better make this look good."

Before she could draw another breath, Jayk swept her into his arms and carried her across the threshold of the room. The tingling current returned with twice the intensity.

Still holding her in his arms, Jayk lowered his head and claimed her lips in a searing kiss. Fire burned through Kelly's limbs as a delicious weakness invaded her. *This is insane,* her mind shouted. All coherent thought fled, but finally the sound of a throat being cleared penetrated. As Jayk set her down gently, Kelly murmured a soft protest. Almost reaching for him again, she saw the bellboy watching them, and she stepped quickly away.

With pink staining her cheeks, she walked across the room to stare out the window. A small waterfall splashed across the grayish rocks and its soothing splash calmed her unexpected rush of emotions. After the bellboy gave Jayk a message, the door closed with an echoing click. She waited through a long silence to see what would happen next.

"Guess we had better get to work," Jayk finally muttered. He deposited both their suitcases on the luggage rack and zipped his bag open. A devilish grin crossed his face and he stopped unpacking. Turning to Kelly, who was still staring out the window, he tried to sober his expression.

"I'll flip you for the couch."

Kelly blinked and turned to stare at him. "You're too tall for the couch. I'll take it — you take the bed."

He just smiled, receiving exactly the answer he'd wanted. Too many times, officers in this situation used the case as an excuse to share a bed. Maybe Kelly was different. Maybe there was a chance for them to build something resembling a partnership. "Let's get unpacked. I want to check the layout of the hotel before lunch."

Later, over an intimate-looking lunch in a quiet corner of the dining room, Jayk actually revealed a bit more of the case to Kelly. Slipping a picture across the table, he began to outline what he hoped to accomplish over the next two days.

"This man is going to meet someone here between now and Sunday evening. I hope to get near him and find a reason to arrest him before he passes off what I'm after. He'll probably be armed and I doubt he has a permit for the gun, so finding an excuse to arrest him may be the easy part. It would be a nice bonus if I also got his contact."

"Just what is it we're after?" Kelly toyed with her salad.

Jayk frowned as if she were impertinent, then he sighed. "Papers." At her glare, he elaborated a little. "Invoices and some security information on a planned theft."

Kelly was still completely in the dark about the case they were involved in, but she didn't want to show any more curiosity. She refused to force herself on Jayk. With a little time and a lot of luck, he'd learn to trust her. From what she'd seen, he was a good cop. So was she. Together they could make one heck of a team.

Jumping slightly as he reached across the

table to hold her hand, Kelly raised surprised eyes to see a loving expression on his face. She knew it wasn't real, but she hadn't expected such intensity.

"We're much too serious. Loosen up and try to look like you're having fun," he told her quietly.

Kelly's laugh was a little too loud. This was ridiculous. They disliked each other. They distrusted each other. They simply didn't get along. But the shivers running up her arm told a different story.

Jumping up from the table, she broke the disturbing contact. She made up an excuse that she had to powder her nose, and she hurried away. A few minutes alone in their room would help her get her perspective back. If they spent the afternoon at the pool, there would be enough people around to keep everything businesslike. Kelly smothered a laugh at the term she'd used. Being on a honeymoon couldn't be classified as business, could it?

Jayk followed absentmindedly, thinking about Kelly. He didn't want to, but he couldn't seem to help it. That kiss they'd shared had rocked the foundations of his carefully structured world. Content with the life he'd laid out for himself, Jayk was unsettled by the thought of any changes.

He was forced to admit that Kelly was becoming an obsession. He couldn't get her off his mind. At odd moments, he'd see her flashing green eyes or her wild curls. Her rippling laughter would ring in his ears and her soothing voice would float through the air. The restlessness he'd felt lately was developing into an aching loneliness.

After what should have been a pleasant afternoon at the pool, they returned to their room to get ready for dinner. Jayk had spent the time studying Kelly from behind his dark glasses, trying to glean a clue about the true person inside. Now wasn't the time to be led by his emotions. He forced all his tender feelings to the back of his mind. He needed to be every inch the analytical, detached police officer to get through this. With that idea firmly entrenched, he settled down to some serious thinking.

Kelly had sensed that Jayk was on edge about something, so she tried to leave him alone. Swimming laps helped ease a little of the tension in her muscles. Feeling some guilt about not living up to her new bride act, she finally decided that anyone watching them would just assume they'd had their first lovers' quarrel.

She quickly dressed for dinner in the decadent bathroom, not wanting to risk a lecture from Jayk on how long it took women to get ready. After almost throwing on her clothes and slapping on her makeup, she sat in one of the overstuffed chairs in the sitting area to wait for him. She felt barely put together, and she was almost afraid to double-check her efforts in the mirror. As a few minutes stretched into ten, she indulged in a private chuckle. He was taking longer in the bathroom than she ever had.

Taking advantage of her moment alone, Kelly called Milly. After hearing hurried reassurances that he was fine, Kelly laughingly let Jimmy return to his game. It left her feeling warm and secure that he was so well taken care of. The twinge of what she might be missing as Jimmy grew up was quickly buried.

Finally, Jayk stepped out of the bathroom, dressed in pants and a shirt. The shirt's top button was undone, revealing a light sprinkling of blond, curly hair. Kelly felt the breath catch in her throat.

Forcing her gaze away, she picked up her purse and slipped her gun inside. She stood gazing out the window, letting the rough beauty soothe her until she heard Jayk clear his throat.

"You look very nice tonight," he said as she turned around. He had a plan for this evening. It was a little screwy, but it should work. But he needed Kelly out of the way for a while. The informant he wanted to meet with was too skittish to have anyone else around. And he knew Kelly well enough to realize he'd have a devil of a time convincing her to stay behind. The first step was to butter her up a little. That wouldn't be hard. She really did look lovely tonight.

"Thank you," Kelly replied stiffly. "Shall we go?"

They walked to the stairs and went down in silence. Just before coming into view of the lobby, Jayk reached for Kelly's hand and tucked it into his arm. The now familiar tingling raced up her arm.

After being seated in the elegant dining room, Jayk ordered drinks. Then he leaned forward intimately and with a soft smile on his face, he began to ask Kelly questions about her career.

The unusual combination of the romantic atmosphere and the impersonal conversation threw her off balance for a minute. Pausing to take a sip of her drink, she collected her thoughts before answering.

Pushing the drink aside, she felt relaxed enough to talk to Jayk like a fellow officer. There was a certain kinship between police officers. Telling a few stories about her early training, she managed to make him laugh. He even added a tale or two about himself.

When the succulent meal arrived, Kelly's drink was replaced with a glass of white wine. She took a cautious sip then set it aside too.

Noticing Kelly's hesitation over the wine, Jayk leaned forward. "Relax," he admonished. "I seriously doubt anything will happen tonight. Besides, we're supposed to be celebrating our wedding, remember?"

As he urged her to take another sip, she became suspicious. "Trying to get rid of me, Jayk?"

Innocence crossed his expression, then he grinned. "Was I being that obvious?"

"Yes." She should have been angry, but instead she wanted to laugh at his lame attempt to get her drunk and out of the way.

He shrugged. "Can't blame a guy for trying."

"I can, and I will. But just this once, I'll let you get away with it. I'll go back to the room after dinner and let you do your sneaking around alone." She pushed the wineglass away. "But this is the last time, Jayk. I expect to be with you from now on. So you'd better warn your informants about me."

He toasted her with his water glass. "Warning taken."

Kelly had fallen asleep waiting for Jayk to return. Stretching slowly, she listened to him sing in the shower. It had been a very strange evening for a supposed newlywed. She'd spent hours pacing the floor, fooling with the television remote, and reading tourist brochures before finally giving up and curling up on the couch.

The shower stopped and Kelly jumped up to grab her bathrobe. She didn't want Jayk to see her in her nightgown.

Minutes later, he stepped out of the bathroom fully dressed, toweling his hair dry. When he looked up, she forced herself to focus on business. "Did you get the information you needed last night?"

He nodded, throwing the towel aside. "How about if we go for a quiet drive into Rocky Mountain National Park? The meeting won't be until later tonight."

"Sounds nice." Kelly smoothed a hand over her hair, hoping it wasn't too messy.

He gave her an indulgent grin as she

reached for the coffee he'd ordered earlier. For the first time in too many years, he found himself wanting to get acquainted with a woman. He still wasn't enthusiastic about a female partner, but for the sake of his case, he'd live with it for now. He was so pleased with his decision, that he didn't even realize what a giant turnaround this attitude was for him.

"Um. . . ." Kelly stood in the middle of the room, her discomfort obvious.

Jayk interrupted. "Why don't I go down-stairs and place an order for room service? We can relax and eat on the balcony," he said, turning to leave.

She called her agreement to his re-treating back. The second the door closed, she hurried to the bathroom, determined to be dressed when he returned.

After a perfect breakfast shared in the crisp morning air, they left for their drive. An occasional word was exchanged during the day-long outing, but Jayk and Kelly were each lost in their own thoughts for most of the time.

After a hearty dinner and another shower, Kelly felt ready to take on the world. Slipping on the ankle holster, she pulled on a pair of black slacks to cover it. She topped this with her loose-sleeved white sequin top. Sweeping her hair up for the evening, she let the soft curls fall as they wished.

When she stepped out of the bathroom, Jayk let out a low whistle. "You sure don't look like a cop tonight."

"Well, I am. So let's go catch some bad guys."

As they settled into a corner of the bar, Jayk started his loving groom act. Kelly still hadn't gotten used to it, and she found herself unsettled by his attention. Giving herself a stern lecture that this was all part of the job, she turned to study the nearly empty room. They had arrived early so they could watch everyone come in.

After half an hour of sipping soft drinks and holding hands, Jayk began to get restless. His foot and free hand began to tap in time to the Western music played by the disc jockey.

"Let's dance." He grabbed Kelly's other hand and tugged.

"We might miss him," she protested.

"Just one or two. It's still too early for a meeting."

Kelly felt a start of surprise as he led her through a lively swing. She loved to dance. However, between her crazy work hours and a poor selection of partners, she rarely

68

got a chance. Now she threw herself into the beat wholeheartedly.

Watching Kelly dance was an experience in itself, Jayk thought as he moved around the dance floor. She was light on her feet and had a good sense of rhythm. He felt regret as the music stopped. Not willing to end his pleasure just yet, he held her back to wait for the next song. As the slow strains of a love song drifted across the floor, Jayk gathered Kelly into his arms in spite of her protests. He wasn't about to miss this opportunity. Good dance partners were too hard to find.

He realized his mistake as Kelly's softness pressed against him. Conflicting emotions stirred within him as she relaxed against him. Soon they both ceased to think, letting the mood and the music weave its spell around them.

As the dance ended, they blinked a few times to readjust to the reality of why they were dancing in a fancy lounge. Reluctantly, Jayk led the beautiful woman at his side to their table. It was getting late. Things should start happening soon.

Taking a thirsty gulp of her soft drink, Kelly looked around the room. Her gaze rested on a man coming in the door, and she stiffened. She grabbed Jayk's coat sleeve to get his attention.

Jayk looked up from his study of the table and saw his quarry. They watched the man walk to the far end of the bar and order a drink.

"I've got to get closer to him." Jayk paused and looked at Kelly. After a long moment, he took a deep breath. "Watch my back, okay?"

She fought the beaming smile trying to light her face as she nodded. This was one giant step toward partnership and trust. She wasn't about to let him down in any way.

Scanning the room, she watched Jayk assume the mannerisms of a drunk and stagger across the room. He was good at playing his part. He bumped into two or three people, mumbling a slurred apology each time. Kelly held her breath when he caught a waitress with a full tray of drinks and tried to dance with her. Maybe he was a little too good.

Deciding she was too far away to be of any help, Kelly got up and weaved her way through the crowded tables. As she scanned the room once more, a man at the opposite end of the bar caught her attention. His face was familiar. Kelly let the image play through her mind as she watched Jayk approach his target.

As her partner drunkenly staggered into his man, using the excuse of keeping his balance to check for a gun, Kelly noticed another movement to the side.

Jayk found the gun he expected and dropped his act. Twisting the man facedown on the counter, he identified himself and quietly began to advise the man of his constitutional rights while easing the gun out of its holster.

The movement Kelly had seen seconds ago materialized into a familiar face. She knew this man from somewhere, but she didn't have time to analyze her memory. Suddenly, the second man moved behind Jayk and started snaking an arm around his neck. Kelly's instincts took over and she rudely shoved aside the one person between her and Jayk. This new opponent had just locked his arm around Jayk's neck when Kelly came up behind him. Before Jayk could react to the unseen threat, Kelly maneuvered him away and he joined Jayk's captive against the bar.

Distracted by the unexpected attack, Jayk momentarily loosened his grip on his prisoner. The suspect took advantage of the situation, slipping out of his grasp. As Jayk tried to restrain his captive again, the man landed a glancing blow on Jayk's chin, temporarily stunning him. Before he could recover, the assailant melted into the crowd and disappeared.

"Are you all right?" Kelly called to Jayk, still holding her prisoner facedown on the bar.

Grunting an answer, he retrieved the gun he'd taken from his missing suspect and tucked it into his belt. He then moved over to handcuff Kelly's prisoner.

All this was accomplished with a minimum of fuss, and few people even noticed what was happening. Jayk quietly identified himself to the bartender and asked for a phone to call for a patrol car to pick up their prisoner. Kelly took a moment to retrieve her purse from the floor. As she stood, Jayk shoved the handcuffed man toward her.

"Meet the patrol car out front while I finish up here," he ordered. "Just try not to trip over this one," he added with a smile tugging at the corners of his mouth.

Kelly's shocked gaze locked onto his face for a long moment before sliding down to his boots. She closed her eyes with a soft groan. Jayk was the officer who had helped with her prisoner that last night on patrol.

Kelly snapped her suitcase shut with a loud click. She felt like a thief, slipping out of the hotel in the middle of the night. But it would be a waste of time to stay the rest of the night. In two hours, she'd be in her own bed, asleep. She just had to survive the drive home in Jayk's increasingly disturbing presence.

Jayk silently moved up behind Kelly and reached for her suitcase. Her slight jump brought a touch of a smile to his serious features. This weekend hadn't gone as he'd wanted, but he could hardly fault Kelly for that. She'd done her part. He had slipped up. It would be interesting to see if her competence held up time after time. Jayk doubted it would. After all, she was a woman.

They checked out and drove down the darkened canyon in silence, each wrestling with their own thoughts. Jayk pulled into Kelly's driveway. Wanting to prolong their time for just another minute, he carried her suitcase to the front porch. She unlocked the door and turned to tell him good night. The words stuck in her throat as she raised her eyes to his. Jayk was watching her with a quiet intensity.

Slowly reaching a hand up to tangle in her hair, Jayk bent toward Kelly. Mesmerized, she watched his lips move closer.

Just as she let her eyes drift shut in anticipation of the kiss, she felt him jerk away from her. With a muttered oath, he strode briskly to his car. Without looking at Kelly again, he sped off into the night.

Chapter Four

Almost stumbling with exhaustion and strangely disappointed, Kelly headed for her bedroom. Pulling her high heels off her aching feet, she indulged in a long stretch. Bed would feel so good tonight.

A loud knock sounded at the front door, causing her to freeze. Cautiously approaching the door, she heard Milly's voice. "Kelly, hurry. I've got to talk to you."

Sensing the urgency in her friend's voice, she snatched open the door. "What's going on?" The expression on Milly's face filled Kelly with dread.

Milly burst into the room and paced the floor. Her forehead was wrinkled with worry and she was actually wringing her hands in agitation. Kelly's stomach knotted. This woman had weathered the usual childhood crises of four children. What had happened to put her in such a state?

Kelly went over and grabbed her friend's arm. "Milly?"

Stopping in mid-stride, Milly turned. "Jimmy's gone."

"What?"

"I think he's run away, Kelly."

"No." Kelly's knees suddenly refused to support her. "He wouldn't!" Falling into a nearby chair, she dropped her face in her hands. He was just a baby. There were so many things that could happen to him. She didn't know what she would do if she lost Jimmy too. He was all the family she had left. He was her little brother.

"After their last TV show, I tucked all the kids into bed," Milly continued, dropping an arm around Kelly's shoulders. "Jimmy seemed awfully subdued, but I figured he was just tired. About an hour later, I went to check on everyone, and he was gone. The bed wasn't even mussed." Milly began to pace again. "He probably just sneaked out the front door. I was busy in the kitchen; I wasn't paying any attention. I ran over here, but I didn't find him, so Bob decided to drive around looking. Kelly, I'm sorry."

Kelly lifted her head and forced back her tears. Now was the time for action, not crying. The sooner she got moving, the sooner he'd be found. "Let's check his room." She stiffened her spine, hoping to shore up her emotions.

She spotted a piece of notebook paper in the middle of Jimmy's bed and snatched it up. She gasped as she sank onto the bed. *Don't worry, Kelly. I've gone to make us rech* was crudely printed on the paper.

"He didn't even spell 'rich' right," Kelly mumbled weakly. A quick search of the room showed that Jimmy's windbreaker and his piggy bank were gone. At the edge of despair, she turned to her friend. "He didn't even take extra clothes. What if it rains? What's he going to eat? Last I checked, he had all of four dollars in that bank. What was he thinking of?" As the tears started to roll, Milly gathered Kelly in her arms, patting her back helplessly.

Forcing the tears away, Kelly pulled back, allowing herself a final sniff. A determined light in her eyes, she wiped her cheeks and squared her shoulders. "Well, he's not getting away with it. I'll report this and get the right people looking for him."

"I thought the police won't do anything for twenty-four hours."

"Sometimes it pays to have friends in the right places." As Kelly dialed the phone, she ordered Milly home. "I'm sure you're exhausted and you've got your own family to worry about. I'll be okay."

"If you're sure," Milly agreed reluctantly. "Bob's still out looking. I'll be right by the phone if you need anything." She quietly left the house.

After a short argument with the desk officer, Kelly convinced him to put out the information. As she recited Jimmy's vital statistics, she had the weirdest sensation. She had taken reports like these dozens of times, but she'd been detached and clinical about the whole thing and mildly sympathetic to the parents. Now it was her turn. It felt strange to answer the questions she usually asked. Why did it have to hurt so bad? Why was she so scared?

Hanging up the phone, she wandered back into Jimmy's room and stood helplessly, trying to take some comfort in his belongings. The little guy was such an innocent. A surprise baby late in her parents' life, he'd been sheltered and spoiled terribly. He'd probably seen something like this on a Disney movie, and he thought of it as one grand adventure, loaded with fun and thrills. Of course, everyone would live happily ever after, just like on TV.

As her panic began to subside, Kelly was racked with guilt. If only she hadn't gone away for the weekend. If only she had been there when he needed her. He might have talked to her, and they could have worked things out. Eventually, she directed her anger toward Jayk. She decided unreasonably that it was his fault for making her be away from home for two nights in a row. Her work took her from Jimmy too much. After all, she was his mother now. Her own mother had always been around when Kelly needed her.

She felt a warm tingle go through her at the memories. Mom had always been there after school to hear about the day, some freshly baked goody in hand. She had always been there to tuck Kelly into bed at night, reading a story or just sitting by the bed. Mom had simply always been there.

Jimmy didn't have that anymore. With the hours she worked, Kelly couldn't give him the attention he craved. Many nights, she came home late and he had to stay with Milly. When she was home, she was often too drained to give him the love he needed. He knew he was loved, she reassured herself. She always made sure they snatched a few minutes together every day, even just for a quick cuddle.

They'd had several long talks since their parents' deaths. Jimmy understood that she loved her work and didn't want to change jobs. At least he always nodded wisely during their talks and agreed with her. Did he really accept it? Maybe he had left because he was unhappy. Maybe he wasn't getting all the attention a little boy required. Or was he looking for the security of a normal family?

Tired of her thoughts, Kelly forced herself to change clothes. Dropping her party clothes in a messy heap, she slipped on blue jeans and an old T-shirt. Slowly, the numbness began to wear off and she felt the beginnings of a burning anger. How dare he do this to her? Jimmy had to know she'd worry about him. Grabbing up her purse, she stomped to the door, prepared to drag her brother home by the ears.

A thought made her hesitate and turn to stare at the silent telephone. What if someone called while she was gone? What if Jimmy tried to get in touch with her? Slowly, Kelly put her purse down and settled into a chair with a heavy sigh, her anger draining away to leave her feeling totally empty.

As she sat there wondering what to do, unwanted thoughts began to creep into her mind. The horror stories every cop dealt with rushed in, almost overwhelming her. Jimmy wasn't equipped to face the harsh realities of the world yet. What if. . . .

The shrill ring of the telephone kept Kelly from completing her thought. Hope surged as she grabbed up the receiver. He'd been found. She let a smile bloom on her lips. Everything was going to be all right. Her hello was breathless and eager.

"Kelly?" The voice was deep and familiar.

The disappointment was like a sharp pain as Kelly recognized Jayk's voice. Blasted cowboy! Surely he could let her have a few hours to herself. She'd just worked with him for two days straight. "What?"

"Could you meet me down at the station right away?" A sigh of frustration came over the line. "The guy we arrested decided he wanted to talk, so I came down. Then he changed his mind and asked for his attorney." Jayk hesitated. "A few minutes later he decided he wanted to talk to the 'nice lady cop.'" Sarcasm slipped into his voice as he said the last words.

Kelly felt a new anger bubble up in her. She just wanted to be left alone. She'd given more than her share to the job. Now it might even cost her a brother. Besides, if she left, she might miss Jimmy. But at least Jayk had asked instead of ordered. After a long silence, she told him she'd be there. It was her job. She'd been called out in the middle of the night dozens of times before. It was all part of being a police officer.

Quickly calling Milly to explain where she would be, Kelly headed out the door. At least this would keep her mind busy. It had only been a few hours, and she already felt as if she couldn't take the uncertainty much longer.

The old car groaned and complained as she started it. As she took the familiar route to work, her eyes constantly scanned the streets, looking for a little blond-haired boy in blue jeans and scuffed-up tennis shoes.

Kelly stepped into the detective division, and Jayk threw her a tired glare. Motioning her to sit down, he handed her a piece of blue paper.

Kelly frowned at the paper, trying to make out the faded words in the dim light. "Looks like an invoice of some sort."

"Nice work, Sherlock. I couldn't have done it without you."

Kelly saved her words and settled for glaring her answer at him. "Isn't Shays Sound Systems one of the companies that lost a big shipment?"

"Yeah." Jayk sat and waited, interested to see what else she came up with. As much as he hated to admit it, those rumpled curls and sleepy eyes hid a clever mind.

"Where did you get this?"

"Off the guy we arrested at the hotel."

Kelly took note of his use of "we" with some satisfaction. Still frowning at the paper, she was silent. Finally she muttered, "I've seen this before."

"What?"

"Nothing," Kelly answered quickly. It was just a loose piece for now, one of those bits of information an officer filed away for future use. Sometimes it fell into place, sometimes it was useless. "Did you call me down here just for this?"

"No." Jayk paused, letting the silence fill the room. "After this guy got done talking to his lawyer, he clammed up." He swung his gaze to Kelly. "Out of the clear blue, he asked to talk with the pretty lady cop who arrested him." Cocking one eyebrow, he gave her a hard stare. "Think you can handle it, sprout?"

Kelly's temper flared. Someday she'd convince this arrogant cowboy that she was a good cop. She could handle this with one hand tied behind her back. "I'll sure give it the good old college try," she answered sweetly. "Where is he?"

"Room three." Jayk put his feet back on

the desk. As he leaned back and closed his burning eyes, images of Kelly began to drift through his mind. Kelly in her evening clothes, Kelly with fire shooting from her green eyes as they argued, Kelly sleepily rumpled in the morning. His feet hit the floor again and he stood in irritation. This wouldn't do at all. She was his partner, a fellow officer, just one of the guys. Nothing more.

Jayk prowled the halls in search of a fresh cup of coffee. Maybe it would be strong enough to prop his eyes open. Even *he* wouldn't drink the stuff sitting in the bottom of the pot in the detective division. It had been standing there for at least two days now. One-day-old coffee would have been okay, but not two. Besides, the hunt would help distract his unruly thoughts.

Carefully sipping the hot coffee he'd begged from the dispatchers, Jayk started down the hall as the door to the interview room flew open. What was she doing? She couldn't possibly be done. Kelly walked into the hall in front of him, not noticing her partner lounging against the wall, watching her.

As a uniformed officer came around the corner, Kelly plowed right into his broad chest. "Whoa there, Kelly," Russ's deep voice carried through the silence as he put his arm across her shoulders. Jayk watched with interest as the two talked in voices too quiet for him to hear, their heads close together.

"I heard about Jimmy," Russ told Kelly. "Is there anything I can do?"

Kelly shook her head silently, fighting the tears that quickly filled her eyes. "I don't know why he ran away. I don't know where to look. And I'm so scared."

"I know, honey." Russ pulled her close. "We're all looking, but you know how that goes. He could be anywhere."

She nodded her head, refusing to let the tears spill over onto her cheeks. "Thanks."

"If there's anything I can do," he offered.

"I'll call," she promised, heading for her office.

"Any time," Russ called after her.

To Jayk, it looked like a very loving exchange. *Forget about her,* he ordered himself. *She's just like all the others. A boyfriend in every port. Any relationship with her would be nothing but trouble.* Angry at his response to this woman, he followed Kelly to see if she'd learned anything. When he walked into the room, he found her slumped in a chair, her head held wearily in her hands. The sight brought him up short.

"Want some coffee?" he asked gently, offering her his cup on impulse. She looked so vulnerable, so totally lost.

"Thanks." Kelly folded her hands around the cup as if she needed the warmth and security.

Jayk fought an uncharacteristic surge of sympathy, reminding himself of the scene he'd witnessed in the hallway. But she looked so forlorn, sitting there in the dim light. "What did you find out?" he finally asked, assuming his usual position with his feet propped up on the desk.

"He wanted a date."

"What?" Jayk bellowed, disbelief covering his features.

"He seemed to think I could get him out of jail and then we could go out on the town. It wasn't put quite that way, but you get the general idea."

He stared at her blankly then laughed. The full, rich sound filled the room and sent earthquake tremors of emotion through Kelly. *I'm just tired,* she reassured herself. Things would be different after a good sleep. Right now, she was exhausted and distraught. All she needed was someone to lean on for a bit. Jayk was handy. Besides, she couldn't be attracted to a cowboy. Especially one who was a police officer.

"Go on home," Jayk told her softly. "I'll take him back to the jail so he can call his attorney again. We'll follow up on Monday."

"To think that I came out in the middle of the night for this," Kelly muttered and slowly left the office. Monday seemed so far away. She would be rattling around the house all day Sunday with nothing to do but worry. There had to be something constructive she could do.

Jayk sat in the pool of light from his desk lamp and watched Kelly leave the room. When she disappeared from his sight, he stared at the empty doorway for a long time before getting up to return the suspect to jail.

Kelly was still on his mind as he started the long drive home. The open window let in the fresh mountain air, heavily scented with sagebrush and pine. The shadow of the mountains in the distance and the tree-lined road never failed to move him, even at night. This morning, in the first stirring of dawn, the silhouetted view was spectacular. Peaks reached into the gray-blue sky, encouraging Jayk to admire what was spread out before him, to empty his mind and point the car for home as he had so many times before. Tonight, it wouldn't work. Kelly kept interfering.

As he puzzled over this woman, his eyes darted back and forth, an old habit from his days on patrol. The flash of a white tennis shoe disappearing around a bush brought his thoughts to an abrupt halt. Stopping the car, Jayk studied the small stand of bushes, certain someone was hiding there. Pointing his headlights into the area, he slipped out of the car, staying in the concealing darkness.

"This is Sergeant Taggert with the Jackson Police Department. Step out into the light with your hands where I can see them."

The only answer was a faint rustling of leaves. Jayk's hand crept slowly to his gun. Once his fingers had curled around it, he tried again. "I said now."

The ominous ring to his voice set off the bushes again.

"Jayk?" The voice was very tiny, very scared.

"Step out where I can see you." Jayk softened his voice, realizing he was dealing with a child.

"Don— don't shoot." With a flurry of leaves, a young boy was expelled from behind the bush. He squinted into the headlights of the car, his arms high in the air.

"Jimmy?"

"Is that you, Jayk?" The tremor of tears was becoming stronger in his voice.

Jayk quickly dimmed the lights and stepped up to Jimmy. Before he could react, the boy flung himself forward, hugging Jayk fiercely. Trying to soothe him, Jayk let Jimmy cry for several seconds before easing him away.

"What are you doing way out here, Jimmy?"

As if suddenly remembering something, the boy stepped back and scrubbed the tears from his face. "I thought I was going the right way, but it was so dark." He straightened his shoulders. "I want to apply for a job as a cowboy."

Jayk watched him quietly. "At my ranch?" When the boy nodded, Jayk squatted down in front of him. "Why do you need a job?"

"Just do."

"Some new toy you want to buy?"

"No."

Jayk studied the boy's face. It still held traces of baby fat. Why would a little guy like Jimmy want money so badly he'd hike across town in the middle of the night? And didn't Kelly even know he was gone? Had she bothered to check on him when she got home? Did she even care?

"Tell you what. I don't need any full-time cowboys right now." Jimmy's face fell. "I'll take you home, and you can get some sleep. Maybe this weekend you can come out and help me clean the barn. I'll pay you for your work."

"But that won't be enough!" Jimmy cried.

"Enough for what?"

Jimmy scuffed his toe in the dirt. "Nothing."

"Is something wrong, partner? I'm a pretty good problem solver."

"I just need a job. A good one. I figured cowboy was something I could do even if I am a little kid."

Jayk frowned. "Get in the car, Jimmy. I'll take you home."

"Do I have to? Don't you know someone who needs help?"

The desperate appeal in Jimmy's eyes tugged at Jayk's heart. "No, Jimmy. Let's go home for tonight. Maybe we can come up with something for you tomorrow."

Jimmy ran into the bushes and retrieved his backpack. Reluctantly he stepped into the car and sat silently most of the way home.

"You hungry?" Jayk asked. Jimmy shook his head.

When they reached the house, Jimmy

bolted from the car and ran up the side-walk. He left the front door swinging on its hinges, a yellow pool of light spilling out on the step. Jayk paused just outside that light, not wanting to intrude but feeling a need to see how Jimmy was greeted.

Staring into the dark, Kelly felt a deep depression settling over her. It would really help to have someone to share this with, someone to comfort her. Milly was a good friend and a big help. But Kelly wanted family close by right now, someone special to share the lonely hours of late night and early morning with, to help her through the long, desolate time just before the sun rose. With the sun came new hope, a fresh approach, a whole new set of possibilities. Night was just the dark promise of despair, of negative thoughts and lonely worries.

An image of Jayk's broad-shouldered build flashed through her head, only to be pushed firmly away. It would be wonderful to have a shoulder to lean on right now, but certainly not Jayk's. She'd have to get through this night on her own.

The bang of the front door made Kelly gasp. She had decided to leave it unlocked just in case Jimmy came home. Was he back or was it someone else?

With no thought for the way she was dressed, Kelly jumped out of bed. When she slipped into the living room, she caught sight of Jimmy, standing uncertainly inside the door. Her heart stopped with the joy of seeing him safe. In less than a second, she was across the room, gathering him in her arms. Jimmy clung to her before pushing away.

Kelly saw the pout of his lips and the tears in his eyes. Her own eyes were watery, but she blinked back the tears. She needed to be strong now, more than ever.

"Jimmy, you scared me to death. Why did you run away?" Kneeling down, she put her hands on Jimmy's stiff shoulders. "Do you want to talk about it?"

"No," Jimmy mumbled in answer.

"I love you, you know. I don't know what I'd do if anything happened to you."

"Probably just go back to work," Jimmy grumbled, jerking out of Kelly's hands.

A stab of uncertainty hit her. "What do you mean?"

Only silence met her question. Sighing in frustration, she studied him for a long moment. They would both deal with this better after some sleep. Her mind was fuzzy with exhaustion, and it was doubtful she could carry on a rational conversation anyway.

"Why don't you head to bed? We can work it out later." Pulling Jimmy's stiff little body into her arms, she gave him another big hug. "Just remember, I love you." She watched him stumble to his room, then she turned to see Jayk standing in the doorway.

"I found him more than a mile west of town," he finally said, stepping inside. "He must have walked all night."

Kelly stared at him, speechless. "What are you doing here?" She wasn't sure she could deal with the cowboy right now. Her emotions were too raw; she was too vulnerable.

"I thought you might like to have Jimmy home."

Kelly glared at him. Was he telling her she wasn't a good sister? "Thank you."

"Is there anything I can help you with?"

"No." Kelly knew she should make some effort to be nice to him. He had brought Jimmy back. But right now she was just too exhausted, too uncertain, and too upset.

"Thank you for bringing Jimmy home. Good-bye, Jayk." Resisting the urge to slam the door on him, Kelly pushed it shut and leaned against it with a sigh.

Maybe she should try to talk with Jimmy again. If something was bothering him, she wanted to work it out now, not let it fester and grow. A peek into his room revealed Jimmy had dropped his shoes, crawled into bed, and was now sound asleep. He was home safe. For tonight that was all that counted.

Kelly sat on the edge of Jimmy's bed for several minutes, stroking his hair, trying to reassure herself he really was okay. Finally, it all caught up with her and she trudged to her own bed. It had been almost twenty-four hours since she'd had any sleep. She would deal with her problems after some rest.

Chapter Five

The old car coughed and sputtered, finally wheezing into the driveway just before it died. Kelly patted the steering wheel in an attempt to comfort the poor thing.

"It'll be all right," she told the car. "When we get back to the station, I'll get you a can of oil and some gas. You'll feel much better." As the car gave one last shudder in answer, Kelly stopped to study her home. The flowers had burst into full bloom and the lawn was green and lush. Last year, she'd finally painted the house, and the exterior gleamed in the afternoon light.

She should be happy and content. A nice home, a good job — even if it was driving her nuts — and a brother to love and raise. It should be enough. But she was frustrated and confused. Jimmy still hadn't told her why he'd run away, and Kelly was beginning to doubt her own abilities to raise him properly. This morning, he wouldn't go to school again. She suspected both problems were interrelated, but she couldn't find the key.

And she had yet to work out a plan for dealing with Jayk. Several ideas had popped into her head, but most of them were illegal, immoral, or would involve giving up on everything she'd worked for.

She'd also hit a dead end on the anonymous phone calls. After some delicate arm twisting, she convinced the phone company to put a drop on her line in an attempt to trace the calls. But first the guy had to phone again.

"Hey, lady."

Kelly smiled a greeting to Milly. "Hi! What are you doing home? Don't you have kids to shuffle?"

Milly laughed as she walked across the lawn. "Billy's sick today. I'm playing nurse, so Bob had to be the chauffeur."

Guilt shot through Kelly. When Jimmy was sick, he was sent over to Milly's house for the day. Milly would took care of him, not her. A small pang of apprehension hit Kelly as she wondered how she'd cope if Milly moved away or no longer needed the extra income.

"Mom!" A pajama-clad Billy hung out the door. "I'm hungry."

"You get back into bed, young man!"

Milly ordered. Rolling her eyes playfully, she turned back to Kelly. "Amazing, isn't it? He has the strength to come get me, but not to walk to the refrigerator. Gotta run. 'Bye." With a wave of her hand, she went back inside.

Kelly stood, wondering if there was a solution to her dilemma. She had to work. They needed to eat. But Jimmy needed more attention. How did a single woman find a happy balance between work and home?

With a sigh, she turned back to the house. If she didn't get the papers she'd forgotten and get back to work, Jayk would have one more thing to growl about. Then again, he'd find something to growl about anyway.

Kelly opened her front door and stumbled to a halt. It looked as if a tornado had gone through the living room. Lamps were tipped over, magazines and papers were strewn about, all the cushions were pulled off the furniture. Two of the overstuffed chairs even lay upside down.

Resisting the urge to double-check the house number to be sure she was in the right place, she stepped inside. She automatically reached into her purse for her revolver. Forcing her shock out of her mind, she let her training take over.

As her eyes scanned the room, her ears strained for any sounds of an intruder. Why would anyone go through her house like this? Every drawer and closet had been thoroughly searched, the contents dumped on the floor and scattered around. What had they been looking for? As she checked out her dresser, she was surprised to see her mad-money jar sitting untouched. Obviously the intruder hadn't been after cash.

Her feet crunched over broken glass. Glancing down, Kelly felt white-hot anger shoot through her. Her mother had collected crystal figurines, which were very precious to Kelly. One lay at her feet, shattered.

Again forcing her anger away, she checked the other rooms at the back of the house. Moving more slowly now, she carefully approached the door to the large hall closet.

Stepping to the side of the door, Kelly reached out and slowly turned the knob. Flinging the door open, she searched the dim interior. The closet contained only its usual jumble of boxes, sports equipment, and winter clothing. Unwilling to admit the intruder might already be gone, she headed for the kitchen. Stopping short, she was surprised to see this room was untouched. Quickly checking the back door, she found it locked. With narrowed eyes, Kelly studied the small pantry. It would be tight, but a man could fit inside.

A noise made Kelly start to spin around, just as a sharp blow landed on the back of her neck. As she fell, her cheekbone hit the corner of the table.

Slipping to the floor, she fought the black-velvet fuzziness threatening to draw her into its soft folds. She had to catch this guy. Finally, she was forced to give up the fight and let her head slip to the floor. Just before her eyes closed, a fancy pair of cowboy boots with silver toe tips moved into her view.

"Let me drop off my backpack and get something to eat. Then I'll be right over," Jimmy called to Mark as they parted at the sidewalk.

"Okay, but we'll have to play outside. Billy's sure to give us his germs otherwise."

Jimmy stepped in the house, whistling tunelessly. Stopping short in the doorway, he looked around in shock. Boy, was Kelly going to be mad when she saw this. Stepping over the clutter, he wondered what to do. Quickly, he made his way through the mess to the phone in the kitchen.

"Kelly!" he cried as he ran across the room. "Kelly?" Jimmy knelt on the floor beside her and touched her face gently. All his fears of the past weeks flooded back, temporarily paralyzing his thoughts. He was going to lose Kelly too. He'd be all alone in the world. If he'd stayed home from school today, none of this would have happened. Jimmy burst into tears, not sure how to help his sister.

In a sudden panic of activity, he jumped up and ran for the telephone. Wiping the moisture from his face, he dialed the police station and asked for Jayk Taggert. Jayk would know what to do. He would take care of Kelly. Bouncing on the balls of his feet, Jimmy almost dropped the phone when he heard a low moan come from Kelly. She was alive! Maybe everything would be okay after all. *Oh, Jayk, hurry up!* he thought.

"Sergeant Taggert," came crisply over the line.

Jimmy's words tumbled out as he tried to explain to his friend. "Jayk, the house is all tore up and Kelly's on the floor and I can't wake her up. Help me!"

Jayk tried to make sense of Jimmy's

words. "Slow down, Jimmy. Take a couple of deep breaths." Pausing to let the boy collect himself, Jayk motioned to another detective. He scribbled a quick note telling him to send an ambulance to Kelly's address before turning his attention back to Jimmy.

"Jimmy, can you tell if Kelly's hurt?"

"I don't know. I can't wake her up," Jimmy cried, his voice starting to quaver. "Jayk, please come. I need you." He dropped the phone, the sound echoing in Jayk's ear.

Jayk beat the ambulance to Kelly's house, breaking several traffic laws on his way across town. As he hurried through the front door, he called for Jimmy.

"In the kitchen, Jayk! Hurry!"

Jayk's mind registered the disarray of the house as he headed down the hall. What was going on here?

"Jimmy, go out front and wait for the ambulance. Direct them in here when they arrive."

"No, I won't leave Kelly."

"The best thing you can do for her is to get the ambulance crew in here. Now go!"

Jimmy left reluctantly, looking back at Kelly several times.

Jayk fought his own panic as he knelt down to take her pulse. Weak but steady, it beat softly against his fingers. Brushing her hair away from her face, Jayk tried to figure out how she was hurt. A red welt was forming below one eye. Other than that, she seemed to be uninjured.

He breathed a sigh of relief. His heart had stopped beating when he saw her sprawled on the floor. It would tear him up if anything happened to this woman. Before he could pursue the meaning of that thought, Kelly began to stir, a soft moan escaping her lips.

As she tried to sit up, a gentle pair of hands held her down then softly stroked her aching head. "Are you all right?" asked a deep voice that rumbled right through her.

"My head feels as if a herd of cattle were stampeding inside. Other than that, I think I'm fine." Letting herself float with that tender touch, Kelly felt almost content in spite of the throbbing pain in her head. How good it felt to have someone take care of her.

"They're here." Jimmy galloped into the kitchen.

Kelly squeezed her eyes tight as his piercing voice tore through her head. The room soon became a whirl of quiet voices, sharp and decisive, as the paramedics checked her over. Unattached hands gently touched her here and there, lights were flashed into her aching eyes, and equipment beeped and buzzed. After answering what seemed like a thousand questions, Kelly was left alone while the paramedics talked to Jayk and decided to take her to the hospital.

"No," she protested weakly. She wouldn't leave Jimmy alone for the night. "No hospital."

Jayk dropped down beside her. "Kelly, you need to see a doctor. You've hit your head pretty hard."

"Twice, no less," she quipped weakly. "I'll be okay. I need to be with Jimmy."

"Kelly, you can't."

"No, Jayk."

"But you —"

"No."

Throwing up his hands in resignation, he stood.

The paramedics reluctantly gave Jayk a list of instructions for Kelly, packed up their equipment, and left. While Jayk talked to them, she struggled to a sitting position, leaning carefully against a cupboard, and pulled Jimmy into her lap. She'd seen the subdued panic on his face.

"You okay?" he asked, examining her

closely. Without waiting for an answer, he draped his arms over her shoulders and gave her a hard squeeze. Leaning back, he blinked to fight back his tears. "You're going to have a heck of a black eye tomorrow. Worse than the one I had last year."

Kelly smiled through the piercing ache in her head. That was the nice thing about seven-year-olds, they kept everything in perspective. Tomorrow in school, he'd tell everyone about his sister's really neat black eye, not about the terror he'd just experienced.

Jayk dropped down to her level once more. "You feel like telling me what happened?"

"Not really," Kelly answered dryly. "But I guess I have to, huh?" Turning to Jimmy, she hugged him and gently urged him away. "Why don't you go play? I need to talk to Jayk for a bit and then I'll come over." Jimmy hesitated until Jayk gave him a gentle nudge.

After the boy left the room, Jayk turned to her. "You're not going anywhere except to bed," he ordered. "Someone will have to stay with you tonight. If you don't have anyone else, I guess I'm elected." At Kelly's refusal, he got a devilish gleam in his eyes. "After all, partners need to take care of each other."

Kelly gave up talking and settled for glaring at him. Talking made her head hurt worse. Maybe he'd take her hint and leave. But she'd forgotten how obtuse he could be.

"Why don't you get up off that hard floor and come lie on the couch? Then you can tell me about all this."

Jayk helped her up and guided her into the living room. He left her leaning against the wall and surveying the room while he quickly put the cushions back on the couch. Kelly studied him in fascination as his shirt moved and pulled, highlighting broad shoulders and smooth muscles. When Jayk settled her on the couch, tucking a pillow under her head, she marveled at how nice he could be when he wanted.

Straightening up a chair for himself, a hard mask slid over his face. "Do you have any idea why this happened?"

"I have a few suspicions." She was trying to figure out where to start her story.

"Would you care to share them with me?"

After a steadying breath, Kelly plunged in. "The day after I transferred to the detective division, I started getting strange phone calls. The man seemed to think I had something that belonged to him, and he demanded I give it back. After making some vague threats, he hung up."

"Why didn't you report the calls to me?"

"I tried. You didn't have time to listen." Kelly took her satisfaction as guilt flickered through Jayk's eyes.

"How many calls have there been?"

"I received one at work and two at home. Maybe when I didn't show up for the meeting last week, he decided to search the house."

"Meeting?" Jayk leaned forward in his chair.

"The night before we went to the hotel, he called me at home. I was supposed to meet him and turn over whatever it is, but I completely forgot about it in all the turmoil. I don't have anything anyway, so it would have been kind of tough."

"Has he ever told you what he wants?"

"No." Kelly sighed in frustration. "When I ask, he just tells me that I know. I have no idea who the guy is or what he's after. I've racked my brain, but I can't think of any of my cases that tie into this." Turning her head toward Jayk, she asked in anguish, "What if he hurts Jimmy?"

Jayk's mouth tightened into a thin line, and a hard light entered his eyes. "He'd better not, or he'll have me to answer to."

His threat was punctuated by a knock on the door. Before he could get up to open it, Milly burst in.

"Are you all right?" she cried as she hurried over to Kelly. "Jimmy said you'd been hurt. What happened? What can I do?"

"I'm fine, Milly. Just a bump on the head." Looking around, Kelly grimaced. "And a trashed house."

"But what . . . ?"

"Can we talk later? My head just isn't up to this."

Milly's calm efficiency slowly returned. "Of course. Jimmy will stay with us tonight. Maybe we can talk tomorrow while we clean up the house."

"Could you stay with her tonight?" Jayk spoke from behind her. Milly whirled around, not realizing someone else was in the room.

Kelly bit back a grin at her friend's appraisal. Milly had a soft spot for cowboys. She looked this one over thoroughly, from the top of his carefully combed hair to his highly polished boots. "Meet my partner, Jayk Taggert," Kelly introduced with a wave of her hand.

"Oh, this must be the cowboy you were talking about," Milly responded, the word 'cowboy' dripping with innuendo. Turning back to Kelly, she smiled naughtily.

Jayk raised an interested eyebrow at Kelly until she looked away in embarrassment. Milly had managed to make her innocent comments about her partner sound much more interesting than they actually were. She could almost see the wheels turning in his head as he tried to figure out what she'd said and how she'd meant it.

Hoping to distract the pair, Kelly answered Jayk's question herself. "I don't need anyone to baby-sit me. It was just a little bump on the head."

Milly ignored her and turned to Jayk. "Shouldn't she be in the hospital?"

"Yeah, but she refused to go. She seems to think she's indispensable here," Jayk replied. "If you can't stay, I'll have to. She needs to be watched at least for tonight, according to the paramedics."

"Hey, remember me?" Kelly waved her hand. "Mature adult, capable of making her own decisions? I'll be fine."

"I need to get dinner for Bob and the kids, and then I can spend the night with her," Milly told Jayk, still ignoring Kelly.

"Okay, I'll stay until you get back."

Turning on his smooth smile, Jayk held out his hand. "Thanks, Milly, that takes a load off my mind. Nice meeting you."

Draping a hand dramatically over her eyes, Kelly heaved a big sigh. "Close the door on your way out, Jayk. I need to get some rest. There's a war going on in my head."

He just studied her with an infuriating grin.

"I'd like to be alone for a while," she said.

"We're not through talking yet. And I'm enjoying your stimulating company."

Switching personalities once again, Jayk continued questioning her. "Did you see the guy who hit you?"

Kelly started to shake her head, but she quickly stopped as daggers stabbed her temples. It hurt to talk; it hurt to move. Couldn't everyone just leave her to suffer in peace?

"No, I was too busy shaking the stars from my eyes."

"Did you hear anything, smell anything? Think."

Running the short scene through her mind, something suddenly clicked. "The boots!" She winced at the sharp pain that bolted through her head.

"What boots?"

"The guy who attacked me had on a really fancy pair of boots. They had silver tips on the toes, with the initials 'TM' engraved on them."

"Another dime-store cowboy." Jayk muttered in disgust. "Well, it's a start, anyway. You don't remember anything else?" At her soft no, he got up from the chair. "Can I get you anything?"

"Some quiet would be nice," Kelly told him shortly, peeved that no one would let her take care of herself.

Silence filled the room after her words. Jayk paced the floor restlessly.

A few minutes later, Milly slipped in the door and whispered to Jayk, "Bob's taking the kids for pizza, so you can go."

With a curt nod, he stepped over to Kelly. She watched him warily.

"You take it easy tonight, and don't come in tomorrow, okay, sprout?"

Kelly's protests died in her throat as Jayk reached out and caressed her cheek with a callused hand. His gaze dropped to her lips and studied their soft fullness for a long moment. When Kelly's bottom lip began to quiver in anticipation, Jayk's tender expression became blank once again and he stepped back quickly.

"Be good, now," he ordered softly before leaving.

Stopping on the top step, Jayk pulled a deep breath of evening air into his lungs. The woman was getting under his skin. He had to put a stop to these feelings. Just now, he'd wanted to kiss her, to offer her his comfort and his strength. Thoughts of Kelly filled his every waking moment and more than a few sleeping dreams. During the day, he'd watch her discreetly; at night he'd try to imagine what she was doing. She was constantly on his mind.

Jimmy walked slowly up the sidewalk. Seeing Jayk, he sat on the step and dropped his chin in his hands. "Is Kelly going to be okay?"

Jayk heard the forlorn distress in Jimmy's voice. The kid needed someone to say everything would be all right, that tomorrow he'd wake up and all this would just be a bad dream. Sitting down beside Jimmy, Jayk tried to form the right words.

"She hit her head pretty hard, Jimmy." Jayk paused and reached over to rest a hand on the boy's knee. "From personal experience, I've found the head is pretty tough. She'll have a bad headache for a few days, maybe be a little more sensitive than usual to the noise boys like you make, but after that, she'll be the same as always." He studied the serious face beside him. "Are you okay?"

"She could've died."

"But she didn't, Jimmy. She's fine."

"If Kelly dies, I'll be all alone in the world. No one will love me anymore and I'll have to live on the streets."

Jayk felt as if he was in a little over his head, so he kept silent while he tried to find the right words.

"That's why I ran away, you know."

"Why's that?" Jayk shifted around to get a better view of Jimmy's face. This kid was awfully serious for his age.

"To get a job. If I could get a good job, I could support Kelly and she could quit work. Then she wouldn't get killed." The quaver was back in Jimmy's voice.

Poor little guy. Jayk's heart hurt for him. He was carrying the weight of the world on his shoulders.

"Very few cops get killed in the line of duty, Jimmy. Kelly should be around for a long time to take care of you." Not knowing what to say, Jayk gave Jimmy a hug.

Pulling away, Jimmy stared at Jayk silently, his eyes wide and a bit fearful. "Do you have to go? I'm not scared or nothin'," he hurried on. "Kelly could use the company."

Jayk forced back the smile that teased his lips and tried to ignore the tugging he felt in the region of his heart. Jimmy was a very special boy, the kind of kid he'd like to have someday. Jayk shoved that thought deep into the recesses of his mind.

"I've got to go catch some bad guys and then go home and feed the horses. Tell you what. This weekend, you two come up to the ranch. While you're there, I can take care of Kelly without her really knowing it. She's a little touchy about that right now. Deal?"

Jimmy's eyes lit up. "Do I get to ride a horse?"

"You bet. All of us will. Maybe I'll even fire up the tractor for you. But it's our secret. I'll tell Kelly later. She has enough on her mind right now."

As he got in his car, Jayk heard the screen door slam behind Jimmy as he ran inside. Wincing at the racket, Jayk felt sympathetic toward Kelly. Starting the car, he pulled into the street, lost in thought.

The urge to protect and care for Kelly had been almost overpowering. It was a very dangerous feeling, in more ways than one. He had to leave, take some time to unscramble his thoughts. He certainly didn't want to get emotionally involved

with Kelly, especially since a sneaking suspicion was beginning to form that any relationship with her would not be of the
temporary kind. He'd vowed years ago not
to subject any woman to a cop's life, and
he wasn't going to change that now. The
problems they'd have to overcome hadn't
changed. His work was important to him,
satisfying a deep need to try to clean up
this world, to make it better for future gen-
erations.

Unless he could get his feelings under
control, they could no longer be partners.
That would be a shame, because Jayk suspected they might learn to work together.
Kelly was only the second officer, male or
female, that he'd ever been able to tolerate
as a partner. He was basically a loner. Sure
they fought half the time; of course he
didn't trust her yet. It was all part of getting to know each other. But the way
things stood right now, if they got into a
bind, he'd be more worried about pro-
tecting Kelly than about doing his job.
That could get them both killed.

The next day, when Kelly stepped into
the division, it was even worse than she'd
imagined. Her eye was now done up in
brilliant Technicolor, so no one could pos-

sibly miss the injury. Fillmore wanted to kiss it and make it better. Another detective offered to go out and buy her a nice raw steak, but then he laughingly decided it was too late. Everyone had a cure from their grandmother or great-aunt that was sure to help, and they all wanted to hear the whole story, complete with the gory details.

Kelly had a terrible urge to make one up. Anything would be more exciting and less embarrassing than the truth. Besides, she was tired of telling the same tale over and over.

By the time she reached her desk, Jayk had worked himself into a cold fury. "I thought I told you to take the day off."

"I'm fine, Jayk, and I have a lot of work to catch up on." Enough was enough. Her head still ached too badly to argue with him. Milly had hurried around the kitchen this morning like a mother hen. Jimmy had balked at going to school, insisting that he wanted to stay home and take care of her. She didn't need more of the same at work.

"I want you to go home and rest, Kelly."

"I will when I get this done," she told him, waving her hand to indicate a stack of papers.

"That wasn't a request, officer." Jayk was

fighting for control. This woman made him angrier than anyone he had ever met.

"Pulling rank again?" She raised her eyebrows.

The pencil in Jayk's hands snapped in two. "Why do you do that? Do you want me to write you up? Are you trying to force some issue here?"

"I just want to be left alone to do my job the way I see fit. Is that so hard to understand?"

"You're still on probation."

"That doesn't mean I have to grovel and worry my way through the day, does it? I *am* still allowed to make decisions and do things for myself. I didn't sign anything giving up my ability to think when I was transferred. Did I miss something?"

Jayk clamped his jaws together and fought for control. She was right. Again. After a long silence, he asked, "Are you feeling okay?"

"I've certainly felt better, but I think I'll survive." She gentled her tone to match his.

Jayk eyed Kelly for a long moment. "Did the lab team go through the house last night?"

"Oh, yeah. Now I have fingerprint powder to clean up too. I'd forgotten how messy the stuff is."

"We'll have their results soon. In the meantime, get your report on paper while it's still fresh. I've got one or two leads I want to follow up." Jayk turned back to his desk and proceeded to ignore her. For the rest of the day, Kelly saw little of him and heard even less. He seemed determined to shut her out and go his own way. This was a new level in their battle of wills.

Shortly after lunch, an arm snaked around Kelly's shoulder and a big hand crossed her line of vision. Her surprised gasp quickly turned into a cry of outrage when she saw what the hand held.

"Didn't anyone ever tell you that you aren't supposed to peek through keyholes, little girl?" Russ whispered quietly in her ear. His hand dropped a doorknob on her desk. "See, if you do," he explained meticulously, "this part of the door usually connects with a vital part of the anatomy and you end up with one of these." Russ touched the side of her face.

"That's not what happened." Kelly tried to look indignant while holding back her laughter.

"That's what I heard. The story is that you were at this massage parlor. . . ."

"Stop," Kelly ordered, her laughter fi-

117

nally escaping. "You idiot. Go away and let me suffer in peace."

An exaggerated pout on his face, Russ looked down at her. "Well, that's almost the story." Sitting down beside her, he looked concerned. "Are you feeling okay? That's quite a shiner you've got."

"It's pretty sore, but I'm fine. Just a little tired of all the harassment."

"Hey, that's what happens when a tough lady like you tackles a rhinoceros."

After she threatened him with her paperweight, Russ left, promising to stop in for lunch one day soon. Kelly returned to her work in a much better frame of mind, glancing up to see Jayk studying her carefully. He had the look of someone with something very serious on his mind. Now what had she done wrong? Her good mood dimmed a bit as she plunged into the dwindling pile of paperwork. She'd lost her will to fight, and she could only hope it would return soon enough for the next battle with her partner.

Chapter Six

"Whoa there, partner." Jayk stretched out his arm to stop the boy streaking past him. "Didn't I hear your sister ask you to do something?" Jimmy stared with sparkling eyes, then a grin split his face. Those eyes were so like Kelly's that Jayk felt a strange twist of feeling grab his insides.

"Yeah, I guess she did. Do I really get to ride a horse?" Jimmy asked, doing an excited little dance.

Jayk laughed and ruffled the blond head that barely reached past his waist. "I think that can be arranged. Go do your chores now." Giving Jimmy a friendly swat on the rump, he tried to hurry the boy along.

As the idea of having Kelly and Jimmy stay at his house had begun to blossom and grow, Jayk found a sweet anticipation had crept over him. The house had been empty too long. He had been alone too long. It was time for those four walls to ring with laughter and rattle with busy footsteps again. Even if it was just for two days.

When he'd hesitantly presented the idea to Kelly, she had flatly refused. Knowing he didn't stand much of a chance of talking her into it, Jayk had resorted to underhanded tactics, and he asked again when Jimmy was around. The boy's excitement and enthusiasm overflowed and after halfheartedly trying to say no, Kelly agreed to the weekend.

Stepping over to Kelly, who was packing the last of the food she'd insisted on bringing along, Jayk studied her. As she turned her head, he glimpsed the remnants of her black eye. He gently brushed his fingers across her cheek.

"Does it still hurt?"

Kelly shied away from his hand like a startled doe. "Only if I squint or laugh too hard."

"If I ever catch up with that. . . ." Jayk stopped and smiled grimly. "Let's just say he'll want to apologize to you."

Kelly felt a warm glow slip through her. She'd been so tough and so independent for so many years. The image she needed to project at work didn't let anyone near. It felt nice for a change.

Shaking off these new feelings, she tried to laugh at Jayk's threat. "My hero," she teased. "Will you protect me from the big, bad wolf too?"

"I suspect you can handle the big, bad wolf all by yourself. You're one tough lady."

Kelly turned away to hide her hurt. She didn't want him to see her tough side. She wanted him to see through to the woman underneath.

Jimmy burst through the door, distracting Kelly from her wayward thoughts. Jayk was equally glad for the interruption. The electricity popping through the air between them was too strong. He felt as if he were about to get burned by sizzling sparks.

"Can we go now?" Jimmy cried as he snitched one last cookie. "I did what you told me, so hurry up, Kelly. We're burnin' daylight."

Kelly laughed at Jimmy's western-style phrase and shoved a sack into Jayk's hands. Grabbing her suitcase, she checked the new dead bolt on the back door. This could be a long weekend. She'd be close to Jayk, in the same house with him for two entire days. Could she take it?

Stopping on the front step, Kelly studied the red Ford pickup in her driveway. She'd read somewhere that real cowboys always drove Ford pickups. Maybe there was some truth to the statement.

"Where's the Camaro?" she asked.

"This seemed more practical for the three of us," Jayk replied easily. "Besides, the trunk of the Camaro would never hold all your things."

Kelly watched the trees flash by. After the hustle and bustle of the city slipped away, she opened her window to let the crisp, fresh air wash over her face. Jimmy's excited chatter blended with Jayk's quiet answers to provide a soothing background for her thoughts. As they drove into the foothills, she felt the tension slowly ease from her body. Up until now, she hadn't realized how much the problems had piled up. The quiet fears she was fighting about Jimmy's problems and the break-in at her house, in addition to her struggles with Jayk, were beginning to eat at her. Reluctantly, she admitted she desperately needed this weekend. The Rocky Mountains rose into view and she turned her attention to the snow-capped peaks.

These two days had been planned for Jimmy. But she needed it too. This was a weekend away from it all, a chance to rest and regroup. She'd treat Jayk as an interesting man, not as the partner she fought with every day. Maybe it was time to get to know the man behind the image, to get under that thick skin and find the real Jayk.

Jimmy's whoop of excitement interrupted her thoughts. As the pickup slowed to a stop, Kelly looked around curiously. She suddenly felt as if she'd come home. Peace and contentment settled over her as she gazed at the clear, blue sky, craggy hilltops, and thick pine trees. Jayk's ranch was a perfect mountain hideaway, nestled in its own private valley.

A huge Irish setter loped over to greet them, his tail wagging furiously. "My, but you're ferocious!" Kelly laughed when the dog began licking her hands. Red jumped up to wash Kelly's face too, almost knocking her to the ground. She pushed the dog down and began scratching his ears. The blissful expression on his face contrasted with the excited twitches of his body as he waited to greet Jimmy.

Jayk came around the side of the pickup, shaking his head ruefully. "I originally bought him as a watchdog. Now I'm convinced that if anyone ever tried to steal anything, he'd help them carry it off." Sensing Jayk was talking about him, Red danced over. "Yeah, I know. You just love everybody."

After an exuberant greeting, Jimmy and the dog headed for the corrals together.

"Don't go inside the fence," Jayk called after Jimmy. The boy had talked endlessly about horses on the drive out here. He'd even clutched a shiny red apple the entire way. Next time he'd want to bring bones for the dog.

"Come on, I'll show you where your rooms are." Jayk filled his arms with suitcases and supplies. He suddenly felt as if he were on his first date again. Where was the smooth confidence that never deserted him? This was just another woman. But he'd never invited a woman friend to his home before, and he wanted to impress Kelly. This was different from an evening of dinner and dancing. That he knew how to handle. This was a whole weekend of living in the same house together, of sharing meals and chores, of being together constantly.

What did Kelly think of his house? Jayk started up the carpeted steps. He saw her looking around discreetly as she followed him. With fresh perspective, Jayk saw how barren it all looked. After their mother had died, he had let his two sisters have all the little mementos and knickknacks, keeping the bare necessities for himself.

Kelly's hand slid over the polished oak banister. She loved this house already. The old elegance of a country home was carefully blended with the practicality of a farmhouse.

"We'll put you in here," he told Kelly as he set her suitcases in the bedroom. "Jimmy's in there." Indicating the connecting door, Jayk stepped over and opened the window, letting in a wave of fresh air.

She silently walked up behind him to admire the view. Together, they watched Jimmy hanging over the fence, trying to coax the horse closer. Jayk turned to ask her a question, but the words stuck in his throat.

Blue eyes met green in a long study. Jayk's callused hand cradled Kelly's cheek. She wanted to pull away, but she couldn't seem to make her limbs respond. This felt so right. His touch thrilled her. *This has to stop*, she ordered herself. There was no answer, as usual.

"Kelly!" Jimmy ran into the house.

Pushing away reluctantly, Kelly walked over to the door. "I'm up here, honey." Footsteps clattered up the stairs and Jimmy skidded into the room.

"The horse ate the apple right out of my

hand," he cried. Before she could respond to his excitement, he turned to Jayk. "Can we ride now, please?"

"Tell you what. You help me unload the pickup and then we'll show your sister how it's done."

The three of them made short work of the unloading, quickly stashing the groceries in the kitchen. As Jimmy began to dash out the door once more, Jayk put out a restraining hand.

"You can't go riding in tennis shoes, partner." Jimmy's face fell in disappointment. Jayk turned away and reached into a cupboard. "See if these will fit." A pair of well-worn boots hung from his fingers.

"Wow, Jayk! Are those for me?" Jimmy dropped to the floor and began pulling off his shoes.

Jayk glanced at Kelly. "I hope you don't mind. They're an old pair of mine."

"No, I guess not," Kelly replied reluctantly. If she wasn't careful, Jimmy would quickly become a miniature version of Jayk. Not that it would be all bad. She was beginning to like cowboys. But Jimmy would be a constant reminder of Jayk if he turned into a cowboy.

"They fit perfect," Jimmy crowed.

Kelly had her doubts about that, but she

didn't want to spoil Jimmy's excitement.

When Jayk pulled out an old cowboy hat and plopped it on Jimmy's head, she laughed. The hat settled down around the boy's ears and he had to peek out from under the brim. Again he insisted it was a perfect fit.

Jayk carefully settled his own Stetson on his head and turned to study Kelly. Kelly felt her breath catch in her throat at the banked fire in his look. Her intuition told her their relationship was about to take a giant step. Was she really ready for this?

"Now we just have to get you fixed up. Think you could be a cowgirl?" Jayk asked softly.

She took a moment to wonder if there was a double meaning in those words. Was he asking her if they could ever find a middle ground? If there was a chance for this spark of tension between them to grow into something more?

"Come on, guys. The horses are waiting." Jimmy held open the screen door.

With a laugh at her little cowboy, Kelly followed him out the door. The back of her neck prickled all the way to the corral.

When Jayk led out a big pinto for her, she eyed it warily. "Don't you have anything shorter?" she asked in a small voice, unwilling to admit her fear.

"You have ridden before, haven't you?"

"Well, sort of."

"Would you care to define 'sort of'?" Jayk raised one eyebrow. "Do you like to ride?"

"It rates right up there with having a tooth filled or getting a tetanus shot."

"Why didn't you say so?"

"I didn't want to spoil Jimmy's fun. He's been looking forward to this all week."

"Don't worry," Jayk assured her. "I'll take him out riding. You just relax. Put your feet up, go for a walk, or whatever. Make yourself at home."

After a quick word with Jimmy, Jayk mounted up and led the boy off for his first lesson. Red hovered between the horses and Kelly, trying to decide where he'd have the most fun. He finally ran barking after the horses.

A short distance across the field, Jayk turned back to watch Kelly. He'd spent too many sleepless nights prowling his property, thinking about her. Cleansed by the moonlight, washed by the mountain breezes, he had finally let go of some of his prejudices. He wanted Kelly in every way a man could want a woman.

She seemed so different from other female officers he'd known; so open, honest, almost innocent. He wanted to give her a chance. This weekend was that time. To trust her as an officer, to have her watch his back time after time, might still be a long way off. She'd have to earn that. But to trust her as a woman was different. He just might be able to do that.

Kelly watched the pair move away, and she saw Jayk stop to look back then ride on. This small respite from his presence would give her a chance to strengthen her armor. The man was getting to her, stirring up emotions she wasn't ready for. Forcing her gaze away from the retreating riders, she studied the forest surrounding her.

She was free. That was certainly a strange feeling. For too many years, there had always been some responsibility hanging over her head. Not that she minded. But there had rarely been time for Kelly, especially since she had taken over Jimmy's care. Every moment of every day was filled to overflowing.

A walk would be nice, she finally decided, one of those carefree strolls with no destination and no set time to return. Setting off at a slow pace, she let her thoughts drift aimlessly for a while. Soon she was totally relaxed.

Sunlight filtered through the trees overhead, providing patchy light and blocking out the blue sky. Dried pine needles crunched under her feet as she followed a small creek gurgling beside her. She recognized a struggling wild strawberry plant. She looked under the leaves hopefully, but it was too early in the season for the tiny fruit. Chokecherry bushes grew in thick clumps, and she smiled at the memory of her efforts to make chokecherry jelly. It hadn't taken long to discover it was more effort than she was willing to expend.

The bumps and rustles of other creatures accompanied her, but she never saw any animals. Her struggles with Jayk, the pain of dealing with Jimmy's uncertainties, even her fears over the phone calls and the attack seemed unreal, part of another life.

Finally turning back to the ranch, Kelly marveled at the peace she felt. The mountains had provided food for her soul.

After meeting back at the house, Jayk, Kelly, and Jimmy ate a quick lunch, not wanting to waste a minute of this perfect day.

"Well, what's on the agenda for this afternoon?" Jayk asked, leaning back in his chair.

"I want to go for a roll in the hay," Jimmy announced.

Both adults stared at him in surprise. Jayk burst into laughter before Kelly recovered. Where on earth had he gotten that from? Too much TV, she decided, nervously joining Jayk in his laughter.

"You got it, partner," Jayk promised. Scooping Jimmy up like a sack of potatoes, he headed for the door. "Come on, Kelly. Let's introduce this boy to hay."

Jimmy's loud protests turned into squeals of delight when Jayk tossed him into a huge stack of loose hay in the barn. Jayk then turned to Kelly, his intent clear.

"Oh, no." Kelly backed away.

"Oh, yes." Jayk grabbed for her.

When he swung her up into his arms, Kelly felt the thrill of being a woman. She knew how to get out of this — an elbow here, a hand there. It was all part of her training. But she didn't want to. Being nestled in his strong arms felt too good. For once, she wanted to forget she was a cop. This was her weekend for that, she reminded herself as Jayk tossed her into the hay.

Jimmy was busily burrowing to the other side of the pile, so Jayk took full advantage of the moment and jumped in beside Kelly.

Wrapping her in his arms when she tried to squirm away, he gazed down at her, his expression unreadable.

"Now this is what I call a roll in the hay," he whispered, bending his head to touch his mouth to Kelly's.

Her insides curled at the brief contact. This was a very different man from the one she saw every day. Unable to resist him, Kelly breathlessly waited for more. As Jayk lowered his head again, a shower of hay fell on them.

"Hey, Jayk," Jimmy cried as he jumped down beside them.

Jayk laughed, a low, deep rumble that went right through her. "Think Red could baby-sit for a while?"

"Am I going to get to see a mountain lion?" Jimmy asked as he launched another armful of hay into the air.

Rolling away from Kelly, Jayk settled on his back and chewed a piece of hay. "No, partner, I don't think so."

Disappointment dropped over Jimmy's face. "Well, how about a grizzly bear?"

"Sorry, but not here."

"Shucks."

A silence settled over them as Jimmy pondered the problem. "Maybe next week we can go to the zoo and see some, huh?"

"We'll see," Kelly broke in, trying to hedge. Seeing Jayk again socially was part of the uncertainty of tomorrow. She didn't want to assume anything at this point.

Supper was a backyard barbecue so they could enjoy the soft evening breeze blowing gently around them. While Jayk grilled steaks, Kelly put out potato salad and the chocolate cake she'd made earlier. Jimmy romped on the grass with Red, putting an edge on his growing appetite.

After the dishes were cleared away, an exhausted Jimmy settled in front of the TV to wind down. Red curled up lovingly at his side.

"Let's go for a walk," Jayk offered quietly, determined to get Kelly alone for a while.

"But, Jimmy —"

"He'll be fine. He'll probably fall asleep in a few more minutes. I'll tell him."

Soon they were wandering through the velvet darkness, silence wrapping around them. This was his chance, Jayk decided. He had her to himself, away from work, away from Jimmy. Now he'd get to know the real Kelly. The soft woman he'd glimpsed occasionally over these past weeks captured his interest, and he wanted to delve deeper. He only hoped he wouldn't be disappointed if he cracked through her tough outer skin and found an empty shell underneath.

"So tell me what makes Kelly Young tick," he ventured.

Kelly looked at him warily, but in the pale moonlight she could only see the outline of his face. What was he up to? The hard, macho cop seemed to be peeking through again. The inner warmth generated by being alone in the moonlight with him warred with the sense of caution triggered by something in Jayk's voice.

"There's not much to tell after the vital statistics."

"Oh, come on." His hand snaked out of the dark to enfold hers. "We all have our little quirks, our likes, dislikes, fascinating stories to tell. What's the real Kelly like?"

She felt herself bristle at his tone of voice. She tried to pull away, but he held fast. Jayk sounded too hard and unfriendly, almost as if he were conducting an interrogation. "Just what is it you want to know, sergeant? Why don't you come right out and ask me?"

Jayk turned her to face him. Obviously, his words hadn't come out right. His growing anger at the disturbing feelings Kelly caused had colored his approach.

Hands resting on her shoulders, he softened his voice. "I like you. I want to get to know you better. Is that okay?"

Slowly, she nodded in response. She wanted him to kiss her. To fold her in his powerful arms and hold her very close, leaving her feeling warm and protected.

As if sensing her needs, Jayk stroked his finger across her cheek, tilting her chin up with a gentle nudge. He traced a path over Kelly's eyebrows, smoothing each delicate curve, before brushing down to close her eyes. He painted a line to the tip of her nose, then caressed her lips.

Kelly opened her eyes and almost gasped at the heat in his gaze. Even though his face was mostly in the shadows, his eyes burned with a potent intensity. Slowly, reluctantly, Jayk turned away and led her back to the house.

At the door, he halted her with a gentle tug on her hand. Turning to face him, Kelly felt her heart begin to race. Jayk bent his head and brushed her lips with his. Kelly reveled in the way her body pressed against his at every point they touched. Reluctantly, she pulled away and opened the screen door. Once inside, Jayk turned off the TV, lifted Jimmy off the floor, and carried him to bed, with Kelly following in a daze.

★ ★ ★

That had been a big mistake. Jayk kicked viciously at a rock in his path. The sun was just coming up and the sky was painted in hues of blazing pink, but he failed to notice the stirring scene. He shouldn't have let his need to touch her overshadow his common sense. But it had seemed so right, so perfect last night. Now his emotions and feelings were a tangled maze.

He'd have to develop a split personality to deal with all this. During the week, he still had to work with Kelly on a professional level. At night, he'd come home to his empty house and remember how right it felt to have her here.

"Good morning."

Jayk watched Kelly climb over a fallen tree. His heart twisted with a foreign emotion, and he made his decision. He had to end this now. Then he could get on with his work and his life. The light sparkling in her green eyes made his resolve waver, but he plunged in anyway.

"We need to talk."

The harsh tone in Jayk's voice halted Kelly. A wary light replaced the sparkle in her eyes.

With a deep breath, he rushed ahead. "You know, Kelly, I'm very attracted to you. You appeal to me in a way no other woman ever has." He turned away from the picture of Kelly, standing with the mountains silhouetted behind her.

"I think you feel the attraction too. But you need to understand there can never be anything permanent between us. Nothing can ever come of it beyond sharing a few magic moments. Do you know why?"

Kelly's only response was a slight shake of her head. Resisting the urge to kiss her soft lips, Jayk fought the twist of regret working through him.

"Between the two of us, we've probably seen more than our share of bad marriages. The first family disturbance I handled as a rookie really shook me up. The woman ended up in the hospital for three days. I couldn't figure out how so much love and hope could turn into that kind of hate. And I vowed it would never happen to me or to someone I loved.

"I also started seeing the marriages of my fellow officers falling apart. Too many perfect, happy couples destroyed by the stress and uncertainty of our job."

He paused, letting the stillness of the forest wash over him. "The song of that siren is in my ears and singing through my blood, Kelly. Police work is my life. I can't give it up. And I won't ask anyone to share this life with me. I like it that way. I have no intention of ever changing. So as much as I'm attracted to you, there's no future for us. We can never be more than partners."

Kelly's sadness at his words slowly turned into anger. He wasn't even going to give them a chance. Last night, she had finally admitted she was strongly attracted to Jayk. And, just maybe, she'd be willing to explore a relationship with him. But he was too afraid to let her into his life.

"There you go again, trying to stuff me into one of your categories." She paced away a few steps. "You're afraid to try, aren't you? You just want to live in your safe bubble and not be disturbed."

In a trembling voice, she added, "I really feel sorry for you. Don't you think I've seen all that too? Don't you think I've had my doubts? I guess I'm the luckier one, because I've also seen good marriages. The kind that get stronger through adversity, where the couple love and support each other, no matter what. If you'd open your eyes and look around, you'd see the good marriages outnumber the bad. In our line of work, we see the exceptions."

Turning away from Jayk to hide the

moisture in her eyes, she glared at the sunrise. "Well, I'm afraid too. I've always vowed I'd never become involved with a cop. But at least I was willing to give us a chance."

She stalked off into the forest, too angry to say more. Jayk wanted to be the lone cowboy, riding off into the sunset at the end of the day. He'd built too many walls for her to knock down. She wasn't even sure she wanted to try.

Jayk stared silently after her. He felt as if he'd just spoiled something beautiful, crushed some unusual wildflower. He'd meant what he said to Kelly. He didn't want to hurt her and he didn't want a long-term relationship with her. At least he was being honest about his feelings. That was more than most men would do for her.

He felt his frustration build as the day dragged on. He and Kelly had called a wary truce for Jimmy's sake, spending the day trying to appease the boy's appetite for ranch life. But the strain was wearing Jayk out. The haunted shadows on Kelly's face tore at his heart, and every time he turned around, he fought the urge to reach out and comfort her. By late afternoon, he was exhausted from his struggles.

The drive back to Kelly's house was accomplished in virtual silence; they all were wrapped up in their own thoughts. Jayk helped carry their bags back into the house, and he stood quietly while Kelly awkwardly thanked him for his hospitality. His return trip home felt strange, out of sync. It was too quiet, too lonely, even with his favorite country-western station blaring in his ears.

Once inside his house, where he'd always found peace and contentment, Jayk felt restless, cooped up. In desperation, he took his horse out for a long ride until both of them were exhausted. Just to be sure he was really tired, he gave his small barn a thorough cleaning, viciously attacking the haystack that held so many disturbing memories.

Later, he still tossed and turned in bed. His body was so tired it ached, but his mind was churning. This weekend had been a big mistake. Instead of dimming, the flames of desire he felt for Kelly burned brighter. It wasn't supposed to happen this way. Images of her frolicking through his thoughts, he finally fell into a fitful sleep.

During supper that evening, Jimmy was very quiet. Then, after they'd cleared the table, he stopped and hugged Kelly so hard she heard a pop in her ribs.

"I'm sorry," he said softly.

"For what, honey?" Kelly set down her load of dishes and crouched down in front of the serious-looking boy.

"For running away. For scaring you."

She pulled him close. "Come here." Abandoning the mess in the kitchen, she led Jimmy into the living room. "All that matters is you're home safe again. But I'd like to know why you left."

Jimmy was silent as he studied her face. "I wanted to get a job."

"Why?" Kelly had expected a million reasons, but not that one.

"So you could quit working."

"I think we'd better start at the beginning." She pulled him back into her arms. "Why would I want to quit?"

"So you'd be safe." Seeing her confusion, Jimmy hurried to explain. "I saw a TV show over at Milly's where a lady cop like you got killed." Tears filled his eyes. "I can't lose you too. I don't want to be all alone."

Kelly settled Jimmy into her lap and let him cry. She'd never suspected he was hiding such fears. Reassurances were easy to give but sometimes difficult to carry out.

When he was done crying, Jimmy leaned back. "I was hiking out to Jayk's. I was going to be a cowboy. If I made enough money, I could pay the bills and you wouldn't need to work."

Kelly felt her heart breaking. What a burden for a seven-year-old to carry. "Oh, honey." She struggled with the tears clogging her throat. "You need to be a little boy first. You'll grow up and go to work soon enough."

Her thoughts racing in crazy circles, she tried to find a way to reassure him. "Police officers don't get killed that often, Jimmy. And I've been well trained. I know how to take care of myself."

"Jayk said that too."

"You talked to Jayk about this?" At Jimmy's nod, Kelly felt the hurt flood through her. She knew the two were growing close, but to have Jimmy tell Jayk his troubles instead of her was almost unbearable.

Silently, she rocked back and forth with Jimmy in her lap, her mind spinning. She felt as if she were losing control. First Jayk, now Jimmy. Suddenly nothing in her life was going according to the careful plans she'd made years ago. And she didn't have the slightest idea what to do about it.

Chapter Seven

If one more thing goes wrong today, I'll scream. Kelly unlocked her car and slid inside with a weary sigh. Leaving the door open to let out the stagnant heat, she pondered the setting sun. It had been a long day, she had missed supper, and she was exhausted. Jayk had finally let her do some minor tasks connected to their case, but she'd gotten nowhere. In fact, she felt like a dog chasing its own tail. Every lead she followed brought her full circle, right back to where she had started.

Deciding it was as cool as it was going to get in the old car, Kelly closed the door and turned the key. Nothing happened. Not even a click. Staring in disbelief at the dusty dials in front of her, she tried again.

"I just don't believe it." Resisting the urge to drop her head to the steering wheel, Kelly quickly reviewed her options. The mechanic had left hours ago. Milly had too many kids at home right now to bundle them all up and come get her. That left begging a ride from someone who was still here. Aiming an angry kick at the car's front tire, Kelly only managed to scuff the toe of her shoe.

The building was hushed and empty. Kelly spotted Fillmore at his desk and reluctantly went over. He'd probably want to stop for a drink. "Are you heading home soon?"

Fillmore glanced up, a slightly harassed expression on his face. "Sorry, babe. I've got to pull this case together for a criminal filing in the morning. I'll be stuck here for a few more hours."

After three more fruitless tries, Kelly wondered if she should walk home. It was four miles, but it would be faster.

Jayk looked up from his paperwork to watch Kelly. He'd heard her asking for a ride, and he knew she wasn't having any success. A little devil inside made him wait to see if she'd ask him. When her gaze slid around the room, touched him, and bounced away, Jayk smiled slightly, ignoring the twinge of pain he felt. She wouldn't. The air between them was still strained.

They managed to work together, but just barely. Acting as if the weekend had never happened, they both relied on an innate sense of professionalism to get them through the days. Being confined together in a car, even for ten minutes, would be too much. Watching Kelly stand helplessly in the middle of the room, Jayk felt his frustration build. He wanted to help her, be with her for just a few minutes. He was a big boy now. Surely he could handle it.

Snapping off his desk lamp, he shuffled his papers together and locked them in his desk. Moving purposefully across the room, he touched Kelly on the shoulder. The energy that flowed from her startled Jayk so much, he jerked his hand away. That special spark between them was still there. When she turned, her green eyes were wide. Apparently she'd felt it too.

"I'm ready to leave now. I'll run you home."

I'd rather not, Kelly's expression said. Her gaze ran around the room once more. Jayk experienced a certain satisfaction at her discomfort. He wasn't the only one who felt as if he were going down for the third time.

"If you're sure it's no trouble," she finally answered.

It would be a total of ten miles out of his way, but it was certainly no trouble. In fact, maybe he could use this chance to clear the air between them — if he used the right words, some magic phrase to explain his feelings. *Good luck, hotshot,* Jayk chided himself silently.

"Jayk?" Lieutenant Goodman stepped out of his office. "I need to talk with you." A weary slump to his shoulders, the lieutenant turned away.

"Relax for a minute. I'll take you home as soon as I'm done." Jayk raked his fingers through his hair in frustration. He'd set a course of action, now he wanted to follow through.

Kelly watched him disappear into the lieutenant's office. Feeling as if she'd been given a short reprieve, she wandered over to her desk and set her purse down. She wasn't ready to spend too much time alone with her thoughts right now. Maybe she could visit someone who was still working.

Wandering down the darkened hallway, she spotted a light in Captain Dunham's office. She stopped by the door, but his back was turned to her, so he didn't see her step inside.

"That's not going to work." The angry words were hissed into the phone. "Those codes weren't easy to come by. Until you find them, we can't move. We'll just have to try someplace else." Turning in his chair, the captain caught sight of Kelly. A red flush covered his face as he fumbled with the phone. "I've got to go," he mumbled before hanging up. "You're working late tonight, Kelly. Problems?"

She watched the captain flounder with his words. Bits and pieces of information fragmented and flew around in her head.

"My car is on the blink. I'm just wasting a few minutes until Jayk can take me home."

"Well, I'm glad you dropped in. I don't get to see much of you anymore."

Kelly noted his voice was too boisterous, his smile too broad. His eyes darted around the room, never really settling on her. Instincts screaming, Kelly tried to find an excuse to stay a few more minutes. The ringing of the telephone interrupted.

Noting the captain's guilty start, she waved goodbye. "I'll stop by again when you're not so busy."

Moving down the hall, she turned and tiptoed back to the door. This was rather late in the day for so many business calls. Either his wife wanted a loaf of bread, or the conversation was something Kelly needed to hear.

"You're going to have to quit calling me here," Dunham muttered. "I know it'll be awkward, but I can't afford to be overheard. Yeah, I'll meet you in about fifteen minutes in the usual spot. Okay."

When the captain put down the phone, Kelly scooted down the hall. She was back in the detective division, looking properly bored, by the time he walked by the door.

"Good night," Kelly called to him.

She needed to move fast, before he had a chance to get out of the parking lot. Kelly started for the door, only to stop in frustration. How could she follow him without a car? Her gaze drifted across Jayk's desk, where the shine of a set of keys caught her eye. No, she couldn't. Jayk would never forgive her. But it was an emergency; this could be a chance to get some important information. He wouldn't just be mad, he'd kill her. And she had no choice.

Before she could change her mind, Kelly grabbed the keys. Running outside, she glimpsed the captain's car leaving the parking lot. Her hand shook slightly as she tried to fit the key in the lock. Her adrenaline was pumping from the excitement of the chase and her fear of Jayk's reaction.

The captain seemed nervous. He kept looking in his mirrors and glancing over his shoulder when traffic allowed. Kelly's challenge was to keep him in sight without tipping him off. This was normally a two-

or three-man job, so the cars could keep switching places. It certainly didn't help that Jayk's car was a flashy sports model.

The captain pulled into a rundown area in the industrial park. He stopped the car, got out, and walked quickly away. Parking beside another building, Kelly followed. The poor lighting hindered her efforts to keep him in sight, but it also provided her with much-needed concealment.

A man stepped out of the shadows, and the two were soon involved in conversation. Papers were exchanged and it was obvious some sort of plan was being made. Kelly inched closer, desperate to hear what they were saying. She was so intent, she didn't see the lid of a garbage can at her feet. The other man's profile looked so familiar. If she could just get a little closer. . . .

A loud clank made Kelly freeze. The two men spun around.

"What was that?" Dunham demanded.

"Just a cat or something."

"No, I don't think so. I've had a funny feeling all evening. Let's look around."

Kelly knew she couldn't stay. There was no place to hide. Gently, she eased backward, hoping she'd make it back to the car without being seen. But the captain was circling around the building, and he would soon cut off her escape route.

"Over there!"

"Stop her!"

A loud crash told Kelly one of her pursuers was out of commission, at least for the moment. Now where were the car keys? Digging in her pockets, she ran up to the car. Luckily, the door was unlocked, so she slid inside, hitting the power locks as she slammed the door. With a sigh of relief, she grabbed the keys, which she'd left in the ignition, and stabbed at the accelerator. She winced as the tires bit into the pavement with a squeal. Jayk probably measured the tread every night.

"Sorry, boss. I would have caught her if I hadn't tripped."

Captain Dunham watched the taillights disappear. "That's okay. I know who it was." He paused to think for a minute. "There's a very simple way to take care of this. I'll handle it in the morning."

Jayk paced to one side of the office, made a sharp turn, and paced back over the same path. Where was she? He still couldn't believe he'd been forced to watch helplessly as his car raced out of the parking lot, a very intent and determined

Kelly at the wheel. What the devil was going on? She'd torn off as if she was after someone. But who? Why? He tried to massage the tightness out of his neck muscles as he covered the same patch of floor for the hundredth time. What if she wrecked his car?

Forget the car. Kelly might be in trouble. And there wasn't even a radio in his car. Glancing at her desk, Jayk grimaced at the sight of her purse sitting on top. For the first time in weeks, she'd carried her gun in her purse; now she didn't have it with her.

"Any sign of her yet?" Lieutenant Goodman snapped off his office light. At Jayk's quiet no, he continued. "Patrol has been notified to look for her. I —"

"Where have you been?" Jayk crossed the room and grabbed Kelly's shoulders. She was okay, his heart shouted. As soon as that thought soaked in, he began to worry about his car. "Where's my car? Why did you take it?" Jayk's voice rose a little on each word until he was practically shouting.

"I'll, uh, cancel the alert," Lieutenant Goodman inserted awkwardly. "You two work this out. I'll talk with you in the morning."

The quiet of the room echoed around

them. Kelly glared at Jayk, and he glowered back.

"Get your hands off me," she said flatly.

Jayk scowled at her another second, then released her. Frustrated, he ran his fingers through his hair, leaving it uncharacteristically rumpled.

"I had to follow up on something. It couldn't wait."

"Something on our case?"

"Yes, but it didn't pan out. Just one of those wild leads that pop up sometimes."

"What was it?" Jayk eyed Kelly suspiciously.

"Nothing. Like I said, it didn't amount to anything." She walked over and picked up her purse. "Are you ready to go?"

She wasn't about to share this with Jayk. For one thing, he didn't deserve to know. The good sergeant still hadn't shared all *his* information with her. Besides, she wasn't sure what she had yet, just bits and pieces that didn't make sense. She couldn't go around accusing a police captain of a crime without proof.

Jayk still glared at her.

"Can we please go now? It's been a long day."

With a curt nod, he reached for his keys on the desk. Then he turned to Kelly with a scowl and held out his hand. Feeling sheepish, she handed them over.

Kelly realized she wasn't going to escape his wrath when they stepped outside. Jayk left her standing on the sidewalk while he pulled out a flashlight and proceeded to go over every inch of his car. He checked the interior thoroughly, plucking a few pieces of grass off the floor and seat. He ran his hand across the hood of the car, almost stroking it. Each tire was carefully examined. Even the lights were checked. Kelly was a nervous wreck when he was done, certain that she'd accidentally scratched the Camaro, or worse.

"You scuffed the whitewalls. What did you do, drive over a curb?"

Kelly stared at him in disbelief. She'd scuffed the tires. That was all? Was that a crime in his eyes? When she just shook her head, he grumbled before ordering her to get in, mumbling, "Are your feet clean?"

It was the last straw. Kelly turned in the seat to tell him what she thought of him and his precious car. But she was too tired, too confused. The words just wouldn't come. Her mouth snapped shut and she faced the windshield. It just wasn't worth the effort.

The drive to Kelly's house was accomplished in strained silence. As they pulled into her driveway, Jimmy ran out. "Kelly! Hurry up! We'll be late."

"Oh, no." Kelly groaned as she stepped out of the car. "I forgot all about this." The turmoil of the evening had completely shoved the memory of Jimmy's Cub Scout meeting from her thoughts. "I'm ready. Get in the car." They'd have to take her old Volkswagen tonight. Hopefully it would start. "Thanks for the ride, Jayk," she called, trying to be civil.

Jimmy turned to Jayk with a big grin. "I'm going to get my wolf badge at the Cub Scout pack meeting."

Jayk smiled at Jimmy. "Well, congratulations. You know, I still have my old Cub Scout uniform somewhere." He turned away, adding, "I wish I could see you get that badge." He waved good-bye. "You have fun."

"You can come along!" Jimmy cried and turned to Kelly. "Right, Kelly?"

She was still trying to get the door to the Volkswagen unlocked. "Uh, sure, if he wants to."

Jayk turned slowly and studied Jimmy with a smile. Then he glanced at Kelly, trying to gauge her feelings. Why not? He didn't have anything better to do tonight, except drive home to a barren house with only his confusion and anger for company.

He soon found himself driving a chattering Jimmy and a very quiet Kelly to the school. As he drove, he carefully tucked his anger deep inside. This was Jimmy's special night, and he didn't want to spoil it.

As they entered the large gym, Jimmy became very quiet, reaching for Kelly's hand. She couldn't convince him to join his group, so they all sat together at the back of the room. She frowned as the meeting started. Jimmy was normally anxious to join the other scouts. Was this another symptom of his fears? Or was something else going on?

Suddenly, Jimmy turned to Kelly, wide-eyed and uncertain. "Everyone here has two parents," he told her softly. "I'll have to go up front with just you." Pausing, he sneaked a glance at Jayk. "Could Jayk be my dad just for tonight?"

Kelly looked at Jayk quickly, his grin lighting an "I dare you" gleam in his eyes. *It would just be pretend,* she thought with a touch of panic.

A few minutes later, she was standing proudly behind Jimmy with Jayk at her side.

"Congratulations, Mr. and Mrs. Young,"

the scoutmaster said as he handed them the parents' pin. Kelly blushed. It would be so wonderful to have a man like Jayk stand beside her all the time, to have a man to share the struggles and the triumphs.

Kelly snapped out of her dream world when she noticed everyone moving away. That's all it was. A dream. Her blush deepened when she saw Milly. The other woman gave her a slow wink and a smile.

By the time she'd wandered back to Jimmy and Jayk, the two were lost in a discussion about scouting. Jimmy was telling Jayk what he'd done to get his badge, and Jayk was responding with tales of his own scouting days.

"You promised me a banana split after I got this badge, Kel." Jimmy gave his sister an endearing grin.

"Well, it is a school night," she hedged, trying to avoid the inevitable invitation to Jayk to come along.

"Please, Kelly. I have all my homework done and I'll go to bed the second we get home."

"Okay, but just this once," she relented. This night had put a special sparkle back in Jimmy's eyes. She didn't want to spoil it. "But we have to eat dinner first."

"Jayk's coming too, right, Jayk?"

Kelly threw a wary look at Jayk, but he missed it entirely, concentrating his attention on the excited boy.

"I'll even treat," he offered quickly. He was having too much fun to let the evening end. Being with Jimmy reminded him of all that was still good and innocent in this world. The cynic embedded in his soul needed more of that.

Kelly followed the pair to the car, trying to sort through the confusion in her head. She didn't know how to deal with Jayk. He made her so mad she wanted to scream, but her body betrayed her whenever he was near, and she was slowly developing a grudging admiration for the man. He was a good cop with a gentle heart hidden under his tough exterior. In his own way, he really cared. Shaking her head, she quickly reminded herself that Jayk didn't want the same things she did out of a relationship. She wanted permanence, but he was looking for a fling.

She steered her thoughts back to her troubles at work as they drove through the night. The turmoil she'd stirred up earlier by following Captain Dunham was still with her. To accuse a police captain of a crime was serious business, especially if the charges came from a probationary detective.

No matter what she did, there would be trouble. If she kept it to herself too long, she could be accused of withholding information, or worse yet, be thought of as an accomplice. If she told the wrong person, she could be considered an hysterical nut. If handled wrong, this case might end her career. Maybe after what Jimmy had revealed the other night, that wouldn't be such a bad thing.

Kelly numbly ate her way through the hamburgers and french fries Jimmy had insisted on. She sat quietly through the scouting talk, listened as the boy wound down into silence in the car, and concentrated on ignoring Jayk as much as she could. Jayk carried a sleepy Jimmy inside, slipped him into his bed, and left her alone with little more than a quiet good night.

Later, as she lay in her own bed, Kelly once again mulled over the information she had on their case. Something had been niggling at the back of her mind all evening. As she relaxed and let her mind drift, it came to her in a flash. Mr. Massey. The drunk driver she'd picked up her last night on patrol. He had been the man with Captain Dunham. Strange, but he kept turning up in the oddest places. First at the hotel, then tonight.

Kelly sat up, fumbling with her light switch in excitement. Of course! TM. Those were his initials. Terry Massey was the man who had broken into her house — she was sure of it. But why? What had he been after? Had something happened when she'd arrested him?

With a gasp, she jumped out of bed to dig through her old uniforms. It had to be here. She hadn't had a chance to get anything dry-cleaned yet. Patiently, she dug through each pocket, fighting her growing excitement. When her fingers brushed against a piece of paper, her heart jerked in anticipation. Slowly, she drew her hand out.

Unfolding the sheet of paper, Kelly studied it as she walked back to the bed. Five abbreviated words were neatly typed on it, like some sort of code. Nothing on the paper indicated what the words meant. But they must have been very important, or Massey wouldn't have tried so hard to get them back. If it took her all night, she'd figure out why. Plumping the pillows behind her back, Kelly settled down, staring blankly at the wall as she tried to sort it all out.

Chapter Eight

Jayk watched Kelly walk into the detective division. Once again, his lips burned with the memory of her kiss. She looked tired today. Not as if she'd been up late or worked too hard yesterday, but as if she'd stayed up all night with some sticky problem. Resisting the urge to smooth away the dark circles under her eyes, he forced his gaze back to his work.

Bouncing her pen on the desk, Kelly worried about how to approach Jayk. She had to make him listen to her theories. She was in over her head, and it was beginning to wear away her confidence in her abilities. Her discovery of the scrap of paper and her suspicions about Captain Dunham were too important. She needed help. And Jayk had the contacts and experience she needed.

If he was still mad about last night, it would be a lot harder to get him to listen to her. His short greeting this morning didn't seem like a good start. Maybe some sort of peace offering was needed first. A complete wax job for his car? New tires to replace the ones she had scraped? Knowing she was being ridiculous, Kelly nervously looked over at Jayk, but she couldn't tell anything from his expression. Gathering her courage, she was trying to find a tactful way to invite her partner for coffee when she was interrupted.

"Kelly, I'd like to see you in my office right away."

The harsh tone in Lieutenant Goodman's voice brought her head up. Had Jayk filed a complaint against her? He looked as confused as she felt, she noted. When the lieutenant closed the door behind her with a sharp click and waved her to a chair with no greeting of any sort, Kelly knew she was in big trouble. Last night's impulsiveness could end up costing her more than she'd thought.

"I found this on my desk this morning." Lieutenant Goodman handed her a piece of paper.

Looking at the computer printout, she was surprised to see her name at the top. She quickly scanned the words, her eyes widening in shock. This couldn't be. Kelly looked up, hoping to see the twinkle of a smile on the lieutenant's face.

His expression was grim, his posture rigid.

"This isn't right!" She threw the paper on the desk. "It's pure garbage. None of it is true."

"I verified it myself. A second computer check brought up the same record."

"But it's a lie!" Someone was trying to set her up. Someone was after her, in a very subtle way.

A tired sigh escaped the lieutenant. "I don't know how or why, but there it is in black and white. I have no choice, Kelly. You are suspended from active duty until this is investigated further."

"No!" Kelly jumped up and began to pace in agitation. "It's not true. You have to know that." Bracing her hands on his desk, she leaned forward, desperate to make him understand. "Why didn't this come to light when I was hired? A thorough background check is run on every new officer. Where was it then?"

"I don't know, Kelly. It's there now, that's for sure. A criminal conviction for extortion and kidnapping is no laughing matter. I have to look into it. In the meantime, I can't allow you to function as a police officer."

"Maybe Jayk and I are getting too close to solving our case. For this to suddenly appear, one of us has made someone very nervous. Someone is trying to discredit me."

Silence filled the room as the lieutenant pondered Kelly's words. The ticking of a small clock was the only sound. With each click, she felt her tension grow until she thought she'd explode.

"Our computer system has a high level of security," the lieutenant said.

Kelly let out her breath slowly. "You and I both know any security system can be breached. You have your doubts — I can see it on your face. Let me stay on active duty. If Jayk and I put our heads together, maybe we can figure out what we did to trigger this."

"I can't —"

"Please, lieutenant." Kelly searched for the words to convince him. "Who else knows about this?"

"So far, just the two of us."

"Give me a chance to clear my name. I can't do that sitting at home. Let me at least try."

"Jayk will have to be told," the lieutenant insisted.

Kelly grimaced. She could just imagine what he'd think. "You're the boss."

"Sometimes I wonder." Lieutenant

Goodman frowned. "Go back to work. Let me think on this for a few minutes."

A tiny smile crept over Kelly's lips as she thanked the lieutenant. Shaky and exhausted from the ordeal, she returned to her desk, where she flopped into the chair. Her relief was slowly replaced by a deep fear. She had really stirred someone up. Was it Captain Dunham? Whoever it was had hit back quickly and deviously. Was she in danger? Worse yet, was Jimmy in any danger? These people had broken into her home once.

Staring blankly at the papers on her desk, Kelly finally forced her eyes to focus on her work. The case. The phone calls. The paper in her uniform pocket. It was all related. And now someone wanted her out of the way. She needed help.

Studying Kelly over his paperwork, Jayk worried quietly. First she had arrived with dark circles under her eyes. Then she came out of the lieutenant's office looking as if she just fought a major battle. He hadn't missed the sound of Kelly's raised voice.

Jayk was just getting up to try to get some information from the lieutenant when his target appeared and called him into his office. Anxious to have his questions answered, he hurried across the room.

"It's a lie," Jayk told the lieutenant a minute later, unconsciously repeating Kelly's words. "I don't believe it." He had his doubts, but partners stuck together. He owed Kelly that much.

"Defending your unwanted partner?" Lieutenant Goodman raised an eyebrow at Jayk. "Strange, but after all the noise you made when I assigned her, I thought you'd jump at an opportunity to get rid of her. Now's your chance, Jayk."

The lieutenant's soft challenge irritated Jayk. He didn't like having his words thrown back at him. "I also don't want her unjustly accused of anything. Kelly's a good cop. That doesn't mean I want to work with her." His words lacked the strength of conviction they had in the past.

"You've worked with Kelly for several weeks now. Do you think she's capable of this?" The criminal record fluttered to the desk between them.

"No." Jayk returned the lieutenant's steady look, resisting the urge to shift in his chair. Something didn't ring true about all this. It was so pat, so convenient. Could it have anything to do with last night? Why now?

"I'm not going to suspend her yet. I want to investigate this further. In the meantime, keep an eye on her." Rising from his chair, Lieutenant Goodman indicated the end of their visit.

Pausing with his hand on the doorknob, Jayk turned back. "I have a hunch someone's trying to set her up." He frowned. "And I intend to find out who it is."

Walking thoughtfully back to his desk, he let his feelings war with each other. Had his subconscious picked up on something he had missed? Was there a reason that his instincts had warned him against any closeness with Kelly? The distrust he'd buried tried to return. Thinking back on their time together at the ranch, Jayk found the charges difficult to believe. Kelly was sweet, warm, loving, almost innocent. Or one heck of an actress.

Stopping in front of her desk, Jayk stood quietly until she glanced up. His thoughtful stare brought a frown to her tired face.

"Let's go for a walk, sprout. You look like you need some air, and we need to talk. Privately."

Kelly meticulously gathered up her papers, tucked them away, and pulled out her purse. Stalling, she tried to control her racing pulse. This was it. Her chance to get Jayk's help. She'd have to take it slowly or he might not listen at all.

Matching her steps to Jayk's, she let the hustle and bustle of the downtown surround them for several blocks. The morning sun tried to warm the cold deep inside her. She looked through the thick trees, hoping to catch a glimpse of the mountains that always soothed her. The thick foliage overhead completely blocked her view, and she suppressed a shudder. All her common sense told her otherwise, but Kelly couldn't help thinking it was a bad omen.

"Did you do it?"

The clipped tone of Jayk's voice burned into Kelly's thoughts. Jerking her head up, she glared at her partner defiantly. "No."

"Do you have any idea how difficult it is to enter a false record into the system?"

"Yes." Kelly struggled with the cloud of depression.

"Why would anyone try to set you up like that?"

The doubt in Jayk's voice finally broke through and Kelly felt her anger bubble over. Stopping, she turned to confront him. "Why would anyone threaten me on the telephone? Why would anyone break into my house? Why am I stuck with you for a partner?"

Jayk's gentle hand pulled her back to his side, contradicting the tightening of his lips. "The all-knowing lieutenant is the only person who knows why we have to work together. It certainly wasn't my idea." Gently, he nudged Kelly forward and they began walking again. "As for the rest of it, your guess is as good as mine. Obviously, you've stepped on someone's toes."

Kelly bit her lip to keep from spouting off again. Taking a few deep breaths, she tried to gather her scattered thoughts. "Jayk, I need to know everything about this case. You've got to share your information with me." A quick glance took in the set of Jayk's jaw, the steely glint in his eyes. "I'm beginning to think your case is related to my harassment. But I need more information." He walked on silently. "I need facts, Jayk. I need your help."

There, she'd asked. The rest was up to him. If he couldn't share the facts of the case with her, then they could no longer be partners. She'd work from her angles and he could pursue his. If it ended her career, at least she'd tried.

"What makes you think what's happening to you is related to the case?" Jayk finally asked, totally ignoring her plea for help.

"Just little things."

Silence once again followed them.

"Not bad, sprout, but you're way off base."

Kelly stared at him in disbelief before turning away and hurrying back to the office. Never had she let a man make her so angry that she lost sight of her final goal. Never had she lost her temper over male prejudices. Before, those attitudes had always served to fuel her determination, making her dig in and try harder.

Forcing herself to calm down, she tried to analyze her feelings. Why did this man send her flying in another direction? Why was he able to ignite her temper? Why was she even worried about it?

And then the feelings exploded over her without warning. She loved him. Kelly Young loved Jayk Taggert. And that put her in an even worse position than she'd been in before.

Kelly stopped and stared blankly into a plate-glass window as she tried to sort through what needed to be done. She'd help Jayk wrap up this case and then get on with her life. They could no longer be partners. That was obvious. The pain of working with the man she loved when that love wasn't returned was more than she could bear. It was probably back to patrol for her. The crazy hours and heavy work load would keep her too busy to think. That didn't solve her problems with Jimmy, but it was the only choice.

She drove home automatically, her thoughts churning with unresolved problems and impossible solutions.

Digging the slip of paper that was her only concrete lead out of her purse, Kelly went into the living room and sat at her desk. Pulling out a pad of paper, she began to doodle, hoping to relax her brain enough for an idea to break through. An hour later papers littered the desk, her eyes burned from exhaustion, and all her brain could concentrate on was Jayk.

Chapter Nine

Kelly had hoped anyone but Jayk would answer the phone. Then she'd just leave a short message and get on with her day. Now she'd have to deal directly with him. "I won't be in to work today. I'm not feeling well," she said.

"What's wrong?"

That was no concern in Jayk's voice. He was suspicious already. She reconciled herself to the fact that he would jump to the wrong conclusions.

"I have a nasty headache. I might be coming down with the flu. I should be back to work tomorrow."

Silence stretched between them. "Afraid to face me?"

"You give yourself too much credit." Just because he was partially right didn't mean she had to put up with it.

"That's what I thought. Well, take care of yourself. I'll try to muddle through without you."

Resisting the urge to slam down the

phone, Kelly hung up carefully. Agitated, she paced across the living room. He was so egotistic, so impossible. And she loved him. The chiming of the old mantel clock alerted her that it was time to get Jimmy off to school. While she listened to her brother's chatter, her thoughts churned. Jayk was actually conceited enough to think she was avoiding him.

Putting her anger aside, she concentrated on getting Jimmy out the door. For once, he went with a minimum of fuss. Leaning against the door frame, she watched him climb into the car with Milly's kids. Jimmy had been happier these last few days. They'd had several heart-to-heart talks since he'd admitted his fears. Kelly was making an extra effort to spend more time with him, even if it was just reading him a bedtime story. The school counselor had been notified of the problem and was trying to help Jimmy too. Yet some fears still lurked in his mind. She'd have to deal with that as soon as she sorted out her own feelings.

As she closed the front door, her anger at Jayk flooded back. Instead of allowing her emotions to paralyze her, she picked up the phone and dialed the first number on her list.

"But is it possible, Chuck?" Kelly listened carefully to the man on the other end of the phone. Frowning, she scribbled a few notes on a yellow pad. "What if a person had the entry codes?" Nodding, she added several words. "It's a big secret. Maybe you'll read about it in the paper next week." Laughing, she put down her pen. "No, it's not illegal." *Maybe not quite kosher, but not illegal.* "Thanks a lot. I'll see you at the meeting next week."

Staring at her scribblings, Kelly tapped her pen on the desk. She was really close. Last night, everything had finally started to fall into place. All those little tidbits she'd stored away were forming a very plausible theory. Now if she could prove it.

Stretching, she decided a short nap was in order. She'd spent the morning on the phone with several computer friends, checking out her ideas. After almost no sleep for two nights, she was exhausted. She wanted to go into the office late tonight, after she was sure everyone had left, to see what she could find. Checking her watch, Kelly saw she had two hours before Jimmy came home. Plenty of time.

A few hours later, waking from her sleep, Kelly looked around the room to see what had disturbed her. Her eyes met Jimmy's. He was standing in her doorway with a worried frown on his face. "Are you okay, Kel?"

Kelly's heart went out to him when she heard the muted fear in his voice. "I'm fine. But I have to work tonight, so I took the day off." Well, that was almost true, her conscience insisted.

Jimmy's shoulders slumped as he turned away. "Oh."

That one little word said so much. Jimmy still felt neglected, and she really couldn't blame him. Her work had intruded far too deeply into their lives lately. Quickly, Kelly jumped off the bed and caught him by the shoulders. When she turned him around, Jimmy nestled into her arms and clung to her.

"It'll get better, pumpkin. I promise. One way or another, it will get better. I'm not sure yet what I'm going to do, but I'll make some changes. I just need some time to figure it out." Holding Jimmy away, Kelly flashed him a big smile. "Tell you what. I forgot to eat lunch and I'm starved. I know you're always hungry. Let's go have an early dinner together."

"Pizza?"

"Whatever you want."

"Could we go to the park too?"

Kelly was pleased to see Jimmy's face brightening. "Do you have homework?" At his emphatic no, she smiled. "Let's do it."

She felt her troubles slip away as she sat on the seesaw with Jimmy. At his insistence, she climbed up the rope tower with him and then competed on the swings to see who could go the highest.

Later, they engaged in a contest to see who could eat the most pizza. While they talked about school and work, Kelly realized this way of life had to stop. They needed more time together. When she'd just been his sister, a little had been enough. Now that she was his mother too, he needed so much more from her.

This past year, she had been confronted with a whole new set of conflicts and responsibilities that didn't fit in with her earlier plans for her life. She needed time to sort it all out, but she was afraid Jimmy couldn't wait.

As they walked home, Kelly had a sudden inspiration. "Jimmy, how would you like a dog?" Maybe some canine companionship would help ease his loneliness and provide a sympathetic ear for his confidences.

"Wow! Could I really?" Jimmy began to dance around her. "Can I have a Great Dane, Kel? Please!"

"Well, I had something smaller in mind." What had she gotten herself into? "I tell you what. I'll make some phone calls, get some names, and we'll check it out."

"Yay!" Jimmy took off and ran the last block of their walk. He was waiting impatiently on the front porch when Kelly caught up. "Just wait until I tell Mark!"

Plans for the new pet filled the moments as they gathered Jimmy's things together. Kelly walked him over to Milly's, dreading this next step. She had one more favor to call in tonight. This wasn't the way she'd choose to do an investigation, but she was desperate. There was simply no other way to get the information she needed.

"Bob, I need your help," Kelly blurted out as she approached Milly's husband on his patio.

"Uh, oh." Bob dropped his newspaper. "This usually means trouble."

"It's not that bad. Just a little computer work."

"Well, that's certainly better than helping paint your house or cutting down a dead tree." Bob pushed his glasses up his nose. "Which almost fell on me, I might add."

Kelly laughed with him, studying Bob's booted feet. His cowboy boots reminded her of Jayk. If he caught her at this, he'd have her job.

"So what is it this time?" Bob's voice was resigned.

"It's a case I'm working on. Someone is stealing shipments of merchandise by computer. I have a few clues and a few ideas. All I want from you is an hour or two of your time to help me sort it out."

"Sounds easy enough. But there's more, isn't there?"

A twinge of guilt flashed across Kelly's conscience. There *was* more, but Bob would never help if he knew. Once he was at the police department, it would be simple to convince him to continue. She hoped.

"Kelly, what are you doing?"

Trying to ignore Bob's stage whisper, Kelly continued to work at the lock on Captain Dunham's office door. She had learned to pick locks in class several years ago, but she was out of practice and she was wasting precious seconds.

Slumping to the floor beside her, Bob

stared at the ceiling. "I'm going to go to jail, I just know it." The silence of the hallway swirled round them. "Why would you break into a captain's office in the middle of the night?"

"I told you. It's for a case I'm working on." Adjusting her cramped legs, Kelly continued to work the pick. Guilt tried to push through her concentration. She had no right to drag Bob into this. If they were caught, he'd be in serious trouble. But she desperately needed his help. She simply wasn't experienced enough to get into the computer system by herself.

"And this captain is concealing evidence, right?"

"This captain may be one of the bad guys."

Bob groaned. "I'm going to be in the middle of it when he barges in here with his machine gun blazing. I love you, Milly. I love you. . . ."

"Oh, stop." The door finally clicked open. "Let's get to work. Go play with the computer," Kelly ordered as she stepped inside. "I need to look for a few things."

"It would help if I knew what I'm looking for."

"Oh, right." She went to the door and glanced nervously up and down the hall.

Turning, she tried to explain her suspicions. "Large shipments of radios, stereos, televisions, and other equipment have been disappearing all over the city. I suspect someone has been breaking into the computer systems of local distributors and generating false delivery records." Kelly threw a pleading glance at Bob. "I think it's being done from this terminal. I need you to get into the system and find any past transactions that don't pertain to police business."

Bob's eyes lighted up with interest. "That's not quite legal, you know."

"Right now, I have no choice. If we're quick and careful, no one will be the wiser and I'll have what I need to finish this case." Kelly reached into her jacket pocket and handed her only concrete lead to Bob. "These may be passwords for someone's system. Maybe they'll help."

Without further comment, Bob went over to the humming machine and began to tinker with the keyboard.

Kelly stepped over to Captain Dunham's desk, frowning. Would he be overconfident enough to leave something that might give him away at the office? If he was receiving phone calls about his crimes here, it was very possible. She opened a drawer and paged through the files.

A few minutes later, she dropped her hands on her hips and looked around. Deep down, she'd known the captain wouldn't make it easy. Glancing at Bob, she saw his frown of concentration, and she decided to look a little further. As she leaned over to check a file folder, Kelly noticed a pink paper poking out from underneath the desk. Eagerly, she snatched it up, her excitement growing as she read. It was an invoice from one of the shipments in Jayk's files.

Stepping over to Bob, Kelly waved a hand in front of his face to break his intense focus. "Yoo-hoo, Bob."

"Huh?" With a start, he glanced up, pushing his glasses back up on his nose.

"Find anything interesting?"

"As a matter of fact, yes." Bob turned to explain his find. "I can only access the last twenty-four hours, but something is going on. Look here." Scrolling through the file, he stopped and pointed to the screen. "Someone pulled up this order and changed the delivery location. Here are the two transactions."

Kelly grabbed her notebook and quickly copied down the address. "When's the delivery set for?"

"Tomorrow, it looks like."

"Bob, you're wonderful." She kissed his cheek.

"How touching."

Kelly jerked around to find Jayk standing in the doorway. She stared at him nervously, trying to force her spinning thoughts into some coherency.

"What is going on here?" Jayk stepped into the room. "I thought you were sick."

Kelly resisted the urge to wipe the palms of her hands on her blue jeans. "A day of rest at home can sometimes do wonders. And there were some things I had to catch up on."

"In the captain's office?"

"I needed to use the computer to check out a theory I have." Kelly shot a warning glance at Bob, who was watching their exchange intently.

"There's one in the detective division, Kelly. Isn't it good enough for you?"

Staring at Jayk, she wondered what she should share with him. She'd wanted to do this on her own, but she'd been caught. There wasn't a lie big enough to cover all her actions. Would Jayk believe her? He had to. The evidence was right there for him to see. Would he let her work on this too, or would he shut her out again?

"I'm waiting for your story, Kelly."

Bristling at his tone, she wanted to fight back, to deny everything. And first thing tomorrow morning, she'd be in front of the lieutenant trying to explain this mess while Captain Dunham packed up and left town. Thanks to her phony criminal record, she'd be suspended immediately. She wouldn't be given the chance to finish her investigation.

"Come look at these computer entries, Jayk."

"I want to know what's going on. Now, Kelly."

"If you'll just listen, you'll find out. Bob, can you bring up that file again?"

"Who's this guy?" Jayk grumbled as he moved to peer over Kelly's shoulder.

"A friend who knows computers." Kelly stopped Bob from introducing himself with a hand on his shoulder.

After one suspicious glare, Jayk turned his attention to the screen. A soft whistle escaped his lips when he started reading the information. "I think you had better sit down and talk to me."

"Bob, put things back where you found them and go home now." Kelly gave him a quick hug. "You've been great. Thanks a bunch. Give Jimmy a good-night kiss for me."

Jayk perched on the edge of his desk. "This had better be good, sprout."

Kelly was too involved in arranging all the information in her head to notice the hated nickname. "Do you remember Mr. Massey, the guy we arrested at the hotel?" Jayk's nod encouraged her to continue. "That's the second time I've arrested him. The first was for drunk driving, my last night on patrol."

"I thought he looked familiar. That was the guy you were lounging on top of when I first saw you."

Kelly shot him a nasty look and continued. "He had a piece of paper on him that I didn't find until after his property was sealed up. I stuck it in my pocket and forgot about it."

She went over to the coffee machine and found that someone had forgotten to turn it off. Pouring two cups, she handed one to Jayk. "Massey was looking for that paper when he broke into my house."

"How do you know he was the one?" Jayk grimaced as he sipped the strong brew.

"Terry Massey. The initials TM on his boots, remember? Also, when I followed Captain Dunham the other night —"

"In my car."

Kelly glared at him. "Massey was waiting for the captain by a warehouse."

"What made you suspect Dunham?"

"I overheard a phone call that sounded odd. The rest I've put together from all the bits and pieces we've collected."

"What's so important about that scrap of paper?" Jayk wandered over to his desk, sat down, and propped his feet up.

Kelly perched on the corner of his desk. "Computer passwords." Jayk's eyebrows shot up. "Somehow Dunham has gotten security codes for some of the big manufacturing companies. I think that's why Massey was at the hotel that night. He went to pick up a new copy of the set I had."

Interest sparked in Jayk's eyes, but he sat quietly.

"Dunham has been using the department computer to break into the systems of major distributors. He'd find a shipment he wanted and reroute it to a temporary warehouse. As soon as he fenced the stuff, the warehouse was vacated with no trace of who had been there."

Finding herself with more nervous energy than she could contain, Kelly began to pace. "In fact, I think I found evidence that he didn't really pay for the warehouse.

He'd rent it, fill out all the paperwork, and get the key. When he was done with that location, he'd break into the building owner's computer system and mark the bill paid in full. But no money ever exchanged hands.

"And look what I found on the floor of his office." She pulled the pink paper from her pocket and handed it to Jayk, who read it silently.

"In his office? Seems like an odd place for a shipping invoice, doesn't it? One that just happens to match up with one of the thefts." The only sound for a long moment was the rattle of the paper as Jayk smoothed the wrinkles.

"No wonder I couldn't pick up on any kind of paper trail," he commented. "Somehow, it doesn't give me a sense of security to know that our world is so easily controlled by others." Silence filled the room as he contemplated the ceiling. "What you did could get this entire case thrown out of court."

Kelly dropped her eyes. "Yes. Fruits of the poisonous tree and all that." Knowing if she didn't, Jayk would, she summed up the Supreme Court decision. "Any evidence obtained by illegal methods is not admissible in court, and any further evidence discovered by those illegal means is also inadmissible."

Jayk watched Kelly quietly.

"I didn't have a choice, Jayk. Who would have believed me if I'd tried for a search warrant? Besides, I didn't think I'd get caught."

"But I caught you."

"It figures."

"I think we can still save the case. All we have to do is catch them red-handed." Jayk stood abruptly. "Good job, Detective Young. This could mean a promotion for you. It'll at least insure that you pass your probation."

Kelly felt a tingle of pleasure rush through her at his words. Praise from Jayk would never just be empty words. He meant it or he wouldn't have said it. Following hard on that feeling was mild dejection. What good would it do her to pass the probation, to get a promotion? She'd still be around Jayk every day, reminded of her love and the hopelessness of it all. And there was still Jimmy.

"We've got some plans to make, sprout."

Suddenly, the nickname didn't sound derogatory anymore. Kelly fought to hold back her smile. Professionally, at least, she was finally making some progress.

"Get me the grid map for the industrial park and let's see what we've got to work with. And a fresh pot of coffee would be a lovely gesture."

"Two steps forward and one back," Kelly muttered as she dug out the requested map. He was finally treating her like a real partner, but he still expected her to wait on him. She tried to console herself with the progress she'd made and not think about the rest.

Two hours later, Jayk leaned back in his chair and indulged in a long stretch. It just might work. Everything seemed to be in their favor. With a tingle of excitement, he realized his months of hard work were about to pay off. And he had Kelly to thank for it. Turning to study her, he noticed how wrung out she looked.

"You look like a walking zombie," he told her cheerfully.

"Thank you. You look nice too." She stared at him. "When was the last time you had some sleep?"

"I took a nap on the desk for a few hours last night. It was comfortable enough." Jayk rose from his chair and switched off the desk lamp. "Let's go home and get some rest. Tell you what. You bring the coffee tomorrow and I'll get some sandwiches. The invoice specified delivery after one o'clock, so I'll pick you up around noon. That will give us plenty of time to get set up." Just before getting into his car, Jayk looked over at Kelly. "You do make good coffee, don't you?"

Chapter Ten

"Coffee?" Kelly held out the thermos. It was all she could think of to break this horrible silence. Their budding partnership had failed in the face of the electricity sparking between them, and they had run out of things to talk about hours ago.

With a slight shudder, Jayk refused her offer. "That stuff was cold and awful an hour ago. No thanks."

Peering wistfully into the dark depths, she agreed. A hot cup of coffee would taste so good right now. She needed something to prop her eyes open. The late-afternoon sun was baking her into a stupor.

Trying to rub the grit from his eyes, Jayk sighed. He'd gone too many nights without sleep; too many nights of dreaming about Kelly, of trying to force her from his mind. This had to stop.

"Is anything even moving out there?" he asked as his head dropped back on the seat. His legs were cramped, his back hurt, and his head was fuzzy with exhaustion.

Not to mention that Kelly was much too close for comfort.

"Not even a cricket."

Almost giddily, Kelly wondered if Jayk would mind if she let out one good scream. From the looks of him, it might help the poor man wake up. Years ago, she'd heard that screaming was a wonderful way to relieve stress. She had to do something. Neither one of them was comfortable, and the tension just kept growing.

She knew the reason for her feelings, but what could possibly be bothering Jayk? The tension was rolling off him in waves. He couldn't suspect. Kelly felt the horror wash over her as she stared blankly out of her window. No, she'd buried her love too deep. No one could possibly see it, so there *had* to be another reason. Swallowing a moan, she leaned her forehead against the glass, taking comfort from the coolness.

"Heads up," Jayk warned in a low voice.

Relieved at the distraction, Kelly watched a truck pull up to the oversize garage doors, honk three times, then pull inside. The two partners watched silently as the driver got out and was met by Terry Massey. The two men exchanged greetings and papers, then they set to work with two other men, unloading the truck.

"I want to go inside and try to see what's happening," Jayk finally said, stepping out of the car.

Kelly got out too, ready to back Jayk up. Meeting him at the front bumper, she was surprised by his next words.

"You stay here." He didn't wait for a response. Knowing he was being unreasonable, he silently argued that he needed his wits about him once he got inside. The distraction of worrying about Kelly would get them both in trouble. It was best if she stayed behind.

Kelly struggled to control her temper. She thought this battle had been fought already. Would she ever convince this man that she was his partner? They needed to work together as a team, and that wasn't possible if she was waiting in the car.

"Hey, cowboy." Kelly paused, making sure she had his full attention. "Fat chance." She pushed past him.

By the time Jayk recovered and caught up with her, she was cautiously easing open a side door to the warehouse. The black interior made her step back, bumping into Jayk's solid chest.

"That was an order, officer," he hissed in her ear as his hands steadied her.

"So fire me," she whispered back,

shaking off his touch. "I'm going with you, like any partner would."

Resisting the urge to resort to caveman tactics and drag her back to the car, Jayk ground his teeth together. Women. They were the most unreasonable, stubborn, infuriating creatures on earth.

As they crept into a dimly lit hallway, Kelly dropped back, letting Jayk take the lead. She'd allow him that much. Maybe it would soothe his male pride. She strained to pick up any sound that would warn her of trouble. All she heard was the soft squish of their shoes.

"Both of you, stop right where you are!"

At that particular moment, Kelly had serious doubts if she could move at all, but her brain was working at high speed. Risking a glance at Jayk, she caught a quick wink from him, apparently to reassure her that everything would be all right. Great. The cowboy was acting as if the good guys always won and this would all be over in time for the next commercial. She hated to be the one to tell him that this was real life and they could get hurt or killed.

Finally, her system switched to autopilot and she began to think like the well-trained cop she was. She still had her gun and her wits. One or the other had often proved to be enough to get out of a sticky situation.

Their unseen captor directed them against the wall with their hands raised above their heads. Something about him nagged at Kelly, so she peaked her shoulder, hoping to see the man's face. That voice was so familiar.

Moving behind Jayk, the man swiftly removed his gun from its shoulder holster, tucking it securely in his waistband. Stepping behind Kelly, he hesitated for a second, as if unsure how to search her.

The man finally reached out and gingerly patted her ribs and waist. Judging her to be harmless, the man stepped back and told them to turn around.

"What are you doing here?" he demanded.

"Sight-seeing," Jayk replied with a guileless smile.

"Sure. Tell me another one." The man turned to Kelly, changing the subject. "I'm still waiting for that little item you were supposed to deliver to me."

"Sorry, but I've been busy working on a case." Kelly's flippant reply belied the touch of fear curling through her stomach.

"So I've heard. If you'd just done what you were told, I wouldn't have had to break into your house."

"How was I supposed to know you were talking about such a small scrap of paper, Mr. Massey?" Kelly felt some satisfaction at the start of surprise in the man's eyes. He hadn't expected her to remember his name.

He waved them forward with his gun. "Let's go see Charlie. He'll know what to do with you."

"What was on that paper that was so important?" Kelly asked, trying to stall for time.

Massey shrugged. "I guess it was computer codes. I'd just picked them up, but I got sidetracked. That was the night you picked me up for drunk driving." Suddenly, he realized he'd said too much. "Now, move."

As they walked, Kelly mused about the irony of it. The phone calls and the terror of having her house broken into were because of a little scrap of paper she would have thrown away if she'd found it.

After several turns, they stepped into the brightly lit warehouse. Kelly and Jayk exchanged glances at the sight of the truck, full of stereo equipment, being efficiently unloaded.

The man called Charlie looked up in surprise and hurried over. "Who are they?"

"Cops," Massey answered.

"Lock them in the storeroom." Charlie turned away. "I don't have time to worry about them now. I've got things to do before the boss comes back. We'll let him decide what to do." With a disdainful glance, he hurried away.

The door of an oversize closet slammed behind them, the key grating in the lock. Kelly took a deep breath to relieve some of the tension coiled inside her, and she looked around. The room contained only a dusty pile of broken, unused office furniture. She muffled a sneeze as Jayk brushed his hand across an old chair, sending a cloud of dust her way.

"Give me your gun," he demanded.

"Why?"

"They've already searched me. At any time Jesse James is going to realize you have a gun too and come back for it. Now give." Jayk held out his hand.

Heavens, the man was starting to make sense. Sliding her gun out of the ankle holster, she passed it over to Jayk. He slid it into his shoulder holster, giving his coat a comforting pat. Maybe he felt better, but she felt naked without a gun.

Eyeing the room once again, Kelly spotted a tiny window about ten feet off the floor. Turning to Jayk, she saw him studying the lock on the door.

"Do you think there's any chance of fitting through that window?" she asked, pointing out her find.

"Well, I guess there's one way to find out." Moving several pieces of furniture, he built a crude staircase.

Kelly leaned back against the wall to watch him work. She hadn't believed it was possible to love one man so much. How was she going to live without him? She'd accepted that he'd never return her love, but that didn't make it any less painful. With a sigh, she forced her eyes away. If they didn't get out of here, she might not have to worry about any tomorrows.

"Nope, too small," Jayk called from his perch. "Not even you could slip through there."

That left only one other option. Kelly hoped she could do it. The lock was a tough one. Slipping up to the door, she listened carefully. Assured that Massey was gone, she pulled a small case from her ankle holster. Removing a slim pick, she went to work.

Jayk settled against the wall to watch Kelly work. This was all his fault. He shouldn't have allowed her to come with him. *And you think you're big enough to stop her?* But she'd be safe now, he argued back. *Right, sitting out in the car, worrying about you.* Would Kelly worry about him? No one had since his mother, and he'd lost her when he was twenty-one.

Now he was worried about Kelly. If anything happened to her, he'd never forgive himself. He'd no longer have a reason to keep trying, to keep hoping. Besides, who would take care of Jimmy?

Unsettled and disgusted by his thoughts, Jayk prowled the room. Kelly eyed him warily as she worked. He was like a caged animal.

About five minutes later, the lock clicked and she stood to ease the door open, checking to see if the hallway was clear. Glancing back, she found Jayk was behind her, peering over her shoulder. Giving her arm a reassuring squeeze, he ushered her into the dim passage.

"Now what?"

"Now we call the cavalry and break up this little tea party," Jayk whispered with a grin.

Kelly almost groaned, but she settled for a grimace. Turning, she caught a flash of movement. Before she could react, an arm snaked out of the shadows to grab her.

Charlie stepped from the shadows and

pulled Kelly tightly against his chest. Cold fear washed over her.

In a well-practiced motion, Jayk trained his revolver on the other man. But not before Charlie pressed his own gun into Kelly's temple.

"Drop the gun, Mr. Policeman," he demanded.

"Not a chance."

"Have no doubts that I will kill the lady, here and now. I have too much at stake to let you get in my way."

"No killing, Charlie." A pale version of Captain Dunham stepped into view.

"There is no other way. Any other alternative will land us all in jail." Charlie twisted so he was able to watch both Jayk and the captain.

"We have enough. Let's just pack up and leave. I've worked with these people, and I won't stand by and watch them be murdered."

"What we've got won't support the lifestyle I'm after."

Listening to the two men argue, Jayk felt as if his insides were freezing. Seeing that gun pointed at Kelly's head forced him to acknowledge his feelings. He now knew that she was one of the best cops he'd ever worked with, male or female. Just as he knew he loved her more than anything else in the world.

His hands began to sweat as he realized he might never have the chance to share his feelings with her. He needed to tell her. *Not now!* The revolver began to slip in his hands as his fear grew. Right now, he needed every scrap of his deeply ingrained professionalism and control. He had to think and react as a police officer. The time for being a man in love would come later, when this was all over.

With relief, Jayk felt a familiar cold control settle over him, just as he watched a change take place in Kelly's eyes. His only chance to save her was coming up.

Hoping she was on the same wavelength as Jayk, Kelly tensed her muscles. Looking steadily at him, trying to warn him of her intentions, she took a deep breath. It was now or never. Hoping her tactic would work the way she and Jayk had discussed one day, Kelly lifted her feet and threw her weight downward, pulling her captor off balance.

As Kelly hit the concrete floor, Jayk simultaneously fired a shot, anticipating her move. He struck Charlie in the arm and the man fell to the floor. Whirling, Jayk trained the gun on Captain Dunham.

Picking up Charlie's gun, Kelly brushed off the seat of her pants, using the simple gesture to try to regain her composure. The two men were quickly handcuffed together in the storage room that Jayk and Kelly had so recently occupied. Captain Dunham was sullenly quiet, while Charlie berated him for losing his nerve.

"Come on, partner," Jayk murmured. "Two down, who knows how many others to go."

As they approached a door in the long hallway, it swung open. They backed against the wall; the open door was their only concealment.

"I'll look around. That sounded a lot like a gunshot. You keep working." When the door swung shut again, Massey was walking down the hall, his back to them.

With a devilish smile and a wink, Jayk glided up behind the man. He definitely watched too much TV, Kelly decided. Jayk tapped the man on the shoulder, then planted a fist in his face. Kelly rolled her eyes toward the ceiling. The worst part was, this craziness was working. Real life just wasn't like this.

"There's one I owe you," Jayk muttered as Massey stumbled backward, hitting the wall. "Here's one just because." As the man crumpled into a heap on the floor, Kelly stepped up with her handcuffs.

A teasing glint in her green eyes, she scolded Jayk. "Two black eyes? Don't you think that's overdoing it?"

"The first one was for all the grief he caused you." Jayk rubbed his knuckles. "Ouch. I'd forgotten how bad that hurts." Retrieving his gun from Massey's belt, he turned. "I'm sure glad he didn't get away with this."

"Onward and upward." Kelly motioned for Jayk to lead the way. "I certainly hope we don't run into too many more. I'm flat out of handcuffs and rope is so tacky." She almost groaned at her words. She had finally cracked under the pressure — that must be it. Her brain was gone. She was actually starting to enjoy this.

Within a matter of minutes, they had rounded up the other hired hands. Kelly tracked down a telephone and they soon had more official help than they could handle. When all the suspects had been taken away, Kelly stood surveying the massive job ahead of them. Everything in this room needed to be inventoried and stored. That in itself was several more hours of work.

It would take awhile for the other investigators to get here. In the meantime, they might as well get started. Rolling up the sleeves of her gray sweater, she started with the closest box.

Gentle fingers eased slowly around her neck and Kelly leaned back into them, letting the strong hands knead her tired muscles. The entire detective division had been opening boxes and making lists all evening. Just another hour and they'd be done. Thinking longingly of her bed, she let her eyes drift shut. "Don't you dare go to sleep on me," a low voice growled in her ear.

"Spoilsport," she mumbled. Her relationship with Jayk had undergone another interesting shift tonight. He was suddenly treating her like a partner, bantering with her as a friend and even asking for her opinion from time to time.

Kelly let her muscles relax. Maybe this was a message from Jayk. Was he trying to tell her this was as far as their relationship could go? That from now on, they were working partners, nothing more?

Jayk studied the dark, tousled curls on Kelly's head and worried as he massaged her neck. He now knew what kind of relationship he wanted with her, and it certainly wasn't just as a partner or a friend.

The trust and respect necessary to be partners was there. He liked her as a friend. But that wasn't enough. He wanted her as his wife. Nothing less would do. But after his stupid speech and her outraged words at the ranch, he was afraid he'd never be able to convince her that she was right for him, even if he persuaded her to forgive him.

Wrapping things up a little later, the two said a quick good night. After a couple of hours of sleep, they'd be back in the office, completing the stacks of paperwork necessary to report this mess and meeting with the chief and the lieutenant to explain it all. There would be a shooting review board to prepare for. But they were ready. They knew what to expect from each other, and they would respond accordingly. After all, they were partners.

Jayk drove toward his ranch, admiring the pink and blue hues of the sunrise reflecting against the mountains. As he drove, he took out his love for Kelly and examined it. He loved her totally — more than he thought possible. But it just wasn't enough. Sadly, he realized he loved Kelly enough to let her go. He'd never subject her to the agony of being a cop's wife. It wouldn't be fair.

Even though she was an officer herself and would understand some of the craziness, it was a difficult life for a woman. The long hours of waiting, worrying that something might happen — it was too much to ask of a mate. The pressures of long hours and high stress could make a man hard to live with. Kelly didn't deserve that.

To give up his job for her would be just as wrong. He loved his work. It had been his whole life for many years. If he gave it up, he'd resent her, and the bitterness would destroy their marriage.

His love would be his secret, held close to his heart. It wouldn't be much comfort during a long winter night, but it was the right thing to do. Now he had to figure out how to get away from Kelly. He certainly couldn't work closely with her day after day. It would hurt too much to be near her.

Chapter Eleven

I've done it, Kelly thought sadly as she watched Jayk laughing with two other detectives. It seemed everyone in the department wanted to talk about their big case today. The two partners had struggled with the paperwork all morning, but they had barely made a dent because of all the interruptions.

But she'd won. She'd convinced Jayk she was a good cop, that he could trust her completely, the way partners do. Last night, they had worked as a well-tuned pair, but this morning it seemed like a very hollow victory. This wasn't what she wanted anymore. She was tired of being one of the guys. It was time to be a woman. A woman in love.

"Hey, Kelly." Russ stood in the doorway, looking like a proud papa. As he moved over to her desk, she watched him sadly. Another friend. They were all just her friends. She'd never find love here. No, that wasn't right. She had found love, but it was one-sided. He'd never know.

"Great job, Kelly." Russ sat in the chair by her desk. "I always knew you were one of the best."

She smiled and thanked him automatically.

"Hey, what's the matter? You should be walking on air right now. That was a pretty big case." Russ leaned forward, concern etched on his face.

"Oh, I guess I'm just tired."

"No, it's more than that. I've seen you 'just tired' before. Come on, give. Don't start holding back on me now."

Kelly quickly ducked her head, but not before Russ caught sight of her trembling chin and watery eyes.

Glancing at his watch, he stood up. "I got off duty an hour ago. Come on, let's get a bite to eat and you can tell me all about it."

"Russ, it's nothing," she protested as she struggled for control. She was so tired. The small portion of the night left for sleeping had been spent grappling with her feelings for Jayk, her despair over the thought of losing her coveted detective status, and her helplessness at dealing with Jimmy's fears. At dawn she was asleep, still sitting up and no closer to any solutions.

"No arguments for a change, Kelly,"

Russ insisted. "We've been through too much together. You never know, I may even be able to help."

Nodding, Kelly grabbed her purse and told Jayk she was going out to lunch. The shuttered mask over his features gave her no clue to his thoughts or feelings.

Jayk watched Kelly leave the room with her friend. He was surprised at the bitter twist of jealousy he felt. He'd hoped he and Kelly would go to lunch together. *Quite a switch for a man who usually never even thinks about lunch,* he thought. He just wanted one last time with her before he began his push with the lieutenant to have her assigned to a new partner. It would make them both happier. It would certainly be easier on him.

Kelly and Russ strolled through the sunshine, enjoying the beauty of the day. Russ took her arm long enough to guide her into a coffee shop, then he dropped it. She was so involved in her thoughts, she could have gone on for blocks.

"Are you sick?" he asked teasingly as the waitress left their table a few minutes later.

"No," Kelly protested quickly. "I'm just not hungry."

"That's a first." Studying her, Russ demanded, "Is it Taggert again?"

"I guess you could say that."

"Right after lunch, he and I are going to have a long talk about you. I can see that idiot will never learn."

"No, Russ. It's not what you think," Kelly said, placing a restraining hand on his arm.

Luckily, their food arrived. From Russ's steady gaze while the waitress was present, Kelly lost all hope he'd drop the subject. With half of his hamburger gone after the first bite, he took up the subject again.

"What's he done to you?"

"He hasn't done anything. Last night, I think he finally accepted me as his partner. I've finally proven to him I can do the job."

A confused frown marred Russ's forehead. "That's what you wanted, isn't it?"

"At one time, yes. Now I want more from him."

The silence stretched between them as Russ pondered her words with a sad shake of his head. "You're in love with him, aren't you?"

At his words, the tears that had burned Kelly's eyes all morning overflowed. As she groped in her purse for a tissue, she nodded. It wasn't supposed to be that obvious.

"Does he know?"

Shaking her head, Kelly sniffed. "And he never will."

"You can't keep working with him. You'll have to transfer and give up your promotion."

"Right again," she answered in a wobbly voice. "Even if I could get the lieutenant to assign me to a new partner, I'd be around Jayk every day. Not only am I going to lose my dream job, the position I've worked so hard for these last five years, I'm going to have a broken heart. What am I going to do?"

Silently finishing his lunch, Russ puzzled over her problem. "There's another dream out there for you."

"I'm not going back on patrol, Russ. I'm tired of the long hours. Besides, Jimmy needs me at home."

"You're not thinking straight, Kelly. A long time ago, you had another dream. Remember?"

Miserably, she answered no.

"The police academy, Kelly."

Her head snapped up. After a moment, a ghost of a smile played around her lips. Wiping her tears, Kelly smiled. "What would I do without you, Russ? Teaching at the academy would solve so many problems right now. It's perfect."

"They just posted an opening today. That's why I remembered. You'd better jump on it before someone else does. Who knows? It might be good for all of us. With a little luck, you can pass along some of your street savvy to those new recruits. I shudder every time a rookie joins the platoon. Were we ever really that naïve?"

Kelly laughed for the first time that day. "I'm afraid we were. Only for a day or two, though."

Picking up her fork, she dug into her salad. At least she wouldn't have to quit her job just yet. There was never much competition for the academy positions. If she could get the transfer, that would be one problem solved.

Walking back with Kelly, Russ pondered her problems. There had to be a way he could help her. Maybe a long talk with Taggert would pay off. Silently, he shook his head. If the man didn't have any feelings for Kelly, any interference would only make things worse. Russ thought back to the times he'd seen them together. Sparks flew. He was willing to bet Jayk acted the way he did out of fear that he might fall in love with Kelly, let her become the most important thing in his life. Now what could Russ do to stoke that fire?

He smothered a grin. Kelly would hurt him for this.

Back at the station, Russ turned to study Jayk, who was watching Kelly. Yes, there was definitely something there. Taggert just needed a shove in the right direction.

"Where have you been? The lieutenant's been waiting for us for twenty minutes."

Here we go again. "I'm five minutes early, Jayk. I told you I was going to lunch."

"Oh. Right." He hadn't meant to jump on her, but that twinge of jealousy was still pricking at him. "Well, let's get on with it."

Quickly stowing her purse, Kelly joined him at the lieutenant's door. It would have been nice if she could have freshened her face and run a comb through her hair first. She felt like an old dishrag. It was the price she paid for staying up most of the night.

"Ah, there they are," the lieutenant said as he shook their hands. "The department's best detective team."

Kelly felt herself flush. She just wanted this over with so she could go home and sleep until next week.

"First of all, I want to congratulate you both on a job very well done. That was a spectacular piece of detective work. Now, I have a confession to make." Jayk and Kelly looked warily at each other as the lieutenant paused. "Jayk, your name has come up several times for promotion, but one thing always holds you back." Finally looking at him, the lieutenant plunged in. "Your difficulty with, or maybe I should say prejudice against, female officers."

Kelly watched a scowl gather on Jayk's face as he opened his mouth to protest. The lieutenant cut him off with a raised hand.

"I know you have what you consider very good reasons. But you're one of the best detectives I've ever supervised. Nowadays, an attitude like yours is career suicide."

Glancing at Kelly, he continued. "The grapevine said Kelly was not only a good officer, but that she was a fighter. Every male officer she'd ever worked with had nothing but praise for her work and her attitude."

Jayk grinned. "I guess your plan worked."

"Of course it did." The lieutenant leaned back in his chair. "Captain Dunham, or maybe I should say Mr. Dunham, signed a complete confession. I still can't believe it." He handed Kelly a computer printout. "This is the only existing copy of your supposed criminal record. Dunham was good. How he planted this in the FBI files, I'll never know. Convincing the Feds to take it back out was an experience I'd rather not repeat."

"Why did he do it?" Kelly had her suspicions, but she wanted to be sure.

"On the night you followed him, he recognized you. He was hoping I'd suspend you, so if you put any information together or tried to make any allegations, no one would believe you. It was a last-ditch effort to discredit you." The lieutenant sighed. "I didn't think you two would talk to each other long enough to put a case together. Congratulations." He stood and shook their hands again.

Jayk held the door open for Kelly, but she hesitated. "You go ahead. I have something to take care of."

When she made her request for a transfer to the academy, the lieutenant tried to talk her out of it. Insisting she was too good to waste her talent teaching, he argued with her for a full five minutes. Finally, he relented, promising her a good recommendation.

When Kelly returned, Jayk set down his cup of coffee and perched on the edge of her desk. She didn't look happy, and he intended to find out what was bothering her. "So, what do we do for an encore, partner?"

"There won't be an encore, Jayk."

His heart lurched in panic. "What do you mean? After last night, passing your probation is a cinch."

"I've asked for a transfer."

"Why?"

"This isn't what I want after all." Kelly fought her panic. *Let it go, Jayk.*

"We make a good team, Kelly." He'd planned the end to their partnership, but he needed to goad her into admitting what was bothering her.

"I know, but I don't want to fight anymore."

"Why not?"

"Personal reasons. I've had enough."

Jayk studied her carefully, but she refused to look at him, pawing through the papers on her desk instead. Something was going on here, but what? If he could just see her eyes, their green depths would tell him. Unfortunately, he was interrupted by the ringing of his phone. Moving over to his desk, he wearily propped up his feet and leaned back to close his eyes.

"Jayk. Russ Burton here. I want to invite you to a party tomorrow night."

"I don't think —"

"This is for Kelly, Jayk, and it would look funny if you didn't show up. The guys from her old platoon want to congratulate her."

"Well, I suppose I could." Jayk's lack of enthusiasm was transmitted over the phone. He wanted the end of this relationship to be quick and clean. His decision had been made, but that didn't make it any easier to be around Kelly.

"That's great. See you at my place around seven. Bring your party smile."

Jayk glared at the phone before hanging up. Just what he didn't need. Glancing over at Kelly, he saw she was still shuffling papers. And she looked worn out.

"Why don't you take off a little early and get some rest. You look beat."

"But this report —"

"Good-bye, Kelly," he insisted.

"Thank you. I am tired and it's been quite a week." She left before he could change his mind.

When Kelly arrived home, she picked Jimmy up from Milly's house and headed for the nearest hamburger joint. She'd made her decision. It was time to share it with him. Maybe the knowledge would help settle his fears. She waited until Jimmy had eaten several bites to appease that constant hole in his middle before she shared her thoughts. "I put in for a transfer today."

Jimmy stopped with his hamburger in midair, his eyes growing wide. "Yeah?"

Nodding, Kelly went on, hoping this would help him. "To the academy. I'll be a teacher, working eight to five, Monday through Friday. No more nights, holidays, or bad guys. Will that make you feel better?"

Eagerly, Jimmy nodded and took a huge bite of his hamburger. "That's great."

His happy chatter on the drive home convinced Kelly she'd made the right decision. Pulling into the driveway, she was surprised to see Russ sitting on her front porch.

"Hi, Russ," she called.

Jimmy hollered a quick hello as he galloped by on the way to Milly's house. Stopping, he came back, gave Kelly a bone-cracking hug, then ran off with a happy grin.

Kelly watched him, a warm glow filling her at having solved this worry. Turning her attention to Russ, she held back a sigh. She was exhausted. His puppylike enthusiasm wasn't something she wanted to deal with.

"The guys want to have a party tomorrow night to celebrate your success. My place around seven."

"Just which guys?"

"The old platoon, of course."

"No one else?"

"Not that I can think of."

Kelly brightened, too tired to pick up on Russ's hedging. "Sounds like fun. It'll be just like old times."

"Did you put in for that transfer today?" Russ stood.

"I typed out a letter just before I left. Let's hope it flies or I'll be back on the platoon with you."

"I don't think I could take that." He rolled his eyes.

The next evening, Kelly dressed carefully for the party in pink slacks and a softly patterned pink blouse, trying to restore her badly flagging confidence. Despite her successes at work, she felt like a failure. At least things with Jimmy would improve when her transfer went through.

Her department-issued car bumped and groaned its way over the wet streets. The weather matched her mood perfectly. When she pulled to the curb in front of Russ's house, her headlights illuminated a white Camaro. Anger rushed through her at Russ's omission, turning quickly into determination. These guys were her friends, and she wouldn't give up an evening with them.

With careful maneuvering, Kelly managed to stay on the opposite side of the room from Jayk for almost an hour. Russ tried to steer her toward her partner several times, but she was too slippery to get caught in his trap.

A piercing whistle shot through the room and everyone turned expectantly to Russ. "For once, we're going to do something at one of these parties besides talk. I've organized a scavenger hunt for you," he announced.

A collective groan ran around the room.

"Hey, gang, if you want eats later, you're stuck." The room grew quiet at the promise of food. "I've divided you up into teams of two. Of course, Jayk and Kelly get to work together to show us how it's done." He started to pass out sealed envelopes.

Kelly looked at Jayk, trying to quell the panic stirring her insides. What was Russ trying to do? He knew her feelings, so he had to know how difficult this would be for her. In his own way, he was probably trying to help. But Russ's schemes often blew up in his face.

"You each have to find one item, but it won't be easy. We'll see just how resourceful you hotshots can be. You have to be back here in an hour or you're disqualified."

"Who's your partner, Russ?"

"I have to get those eats ready. You animals are always hungry. Now get a move on, the clock's ticking."

Grumbles and groans faded into the night until Russ was left alone in a quiet room. He sure hoped this worked. The look Kelly gave him just before she left signified a horrible fate. If things went wrong, he'd spend weeks trying to make it up to her.

"Well, what's this elusive prize we're after?" Jayk pulled the car out into the rainy night.

Kelly tore open the envelope and felt a lump grow in her throat, choking the urge to curse Russ. He knew how she felt about white roses. And in a weak moment she'd shared that feeling with Jayk too. What had possessed Russ to send them after one? The idiot must think he was an overgrown cupid. Kelly could have told him nothing would work. Jayk had firmly shut her out of his life. It would take a lot more than a simple rose to change that.

"Well?" Jayk halted at the stop sign and waited impatiently. "Where to? What are we after?"

"A white rose." Kelly barely managed to say the words.

Panic shot through Jayk. He had been given one more chance, another opportunity to risk his heart. Should he take it? Did he want to live alone the rest of his life? He'd rattled around in the farmhouse since Kelly had been there, feeling the silence closing in on him. That house had been built for love and laughter. Jayk struggled with his love. He needed Kelly to make him whole. Maybe the risk was worth any slice of time he'd have with her.

"Where are we going?" Kelly finally asked halfheartedly. "Do you know a flower shop that's still open?"

Jayk started from his musings. "Flower shop?"

"For a white rose. I know a scavenger hunt is not your idea of a wild time, but Russ will be hurt if we don't make an effort."

He pressed down on the gas pedal. "I know just the place." Yes, it *was* worth it. It was worth any risk.

Pulling up to a darkened shop, Jayk started to get out of the car. Turning to Kelly, he quickly explained. "The owner is one of my informants. He lives around back, so I'll see if he'll open the shop for us. Why don't you wait here so you don't get wet?"

For once, Kelly was more than happy to comply. She watched as Jayk ran through the steady drizzle, sadly forcing her heart to say good-bye to him. A few more days at work and hopefully she'd never see him again. Idly, she looked through the falling rain to see a light flicker on in the back of the small shop. Two figures moved back and forth, talking and gesturing. All this for one rose?

Kelly forced her gaze away. She'd get over Jayk. Always a strong person, she was confident that unrequited love wouldn't do her in. It would hurt for a while, but with Jimmy and a new job to distract her, she'd survive.

When the car door opened, Kelly kept her eyes averted. She didn't trust herself to look at Jayk now, especially not when he was carrying a white rose. She'd told Russ once that the flower symbolized true love to her. Love that was pure and perfect, that could withstand the stresses of life, coming back to bloom fresh and beautiful after each barren and lonely time.

"Here you are."

Jayk's soft voice compelled her to turn and look at him. That strong hand, the one that had touched her so gently, was holding the fragile stem of a perfect white rose. The fragrance seeped into the car, into Kelly's being, making her hope miracles were possible. Tearing her gaze away, she looked at his face and saw a gentle light shining from his eyes. Hope blossomed deep inside her.

Laying the flower in her lap, Jayk reached up and brought another rose into the car. Water drops beaded on the pristine petals like love washed clean of pain and doubt.

Rain dripped into the car, running in rivers down the soft red leather covering the door and pooling at Jayk's feet. For once, he didn't seem to be thinking of his car. A third rose appeared, then a fourth, until Kelly's lap was filled with the fragrant blooms. When Jayk finally pulled the door shut, she raised her gaze to meet his, her heart thudding painfully in her chest. The blue fire in his eyes seared her to her very soul and branded his name on her heart forever.

"Kelly, will you marry me?"

Repeating the words over and over in her mind, she was certain she'd heard wrong.

"Don't say no, Kelly." Jayk took her cold hand, a touch of panic in his voice. "I know how you feel about marrying a police officer. But I love you with all my heart." His silver tongue had never failed him. He desperately called on all his skills to convince her.

"What do you mean?" She needed to stall him until her frozen brain started to function again. He couldn't have possibly said what she'd just heard. She just wanted to hear those words so badly, her frazzled mind had made them up.

"I don't think the question needs an explanation." He squeezed her fingers. "Will you marry me, let me help you raise Jimmy, be the mother of my children?"

At her continuing shocked silence, Jayk took a deep breath. *Don't panic. She hasn't said no yet. Just keep talking.* He had to get through to her. "Kelly, I love you."

"But . . . but your work. You don't want to get married, remember? Your work is your life." The words tumbled out as a warm spot flickered in the very center of Kelly's being.

"It doesn't have to be that way. I've given this job my total attention for nine years. It's time to back off a bit, live for myself for a change. I'll have to make a few adjustments, but we could still have a good life together."

Kelly stared at him while that warm spot grew, blossoming into life, giving hope and love, promising forever. "I didn't think I'd ever hear those words from you. The answer is yes to all your questions."

A look of love and devotion settled over Jayk's face as he pulled Kelly into his arms for a long kiss. She had changed him, made him remember there was good and innocence and, most of all, love still left in this world.

When they finally broke apart, Jayk looked seriously at Kelly before settling her more comfortably in his arms. Now that he had her, he didn't want to let her go. "I think we need to talk." Looking into those green eyes, he felt his insides melt. "First, I want you to know something. My job is no longer my whole life. I've discovered there are so many other things out there that are equally important. You are my siren's song. The one and only real obsession of my life. I love you, Kelly." Jayk leaned forward to seal his promise with another kiss.

Kelly's heart sang its own song as his lips moved gently over hers. She knew her world was finally complete.

Two hours later, the scavenger hunt teams had arrived back at Russ's house, the prize had been awarded, and the party was in full swing. No one seemed to notice that the guest of honor and her partner still hadn't returned. Russ surveyed the room carefully, looked at his watch, and smiled.